STILL WATER

Elizabeth Dickhut

STILL WATER Copyright © 2024 by Elizabeth Dickhut

All rights reserved. Printed in the United States of America. No part of this book may be used or reproduced in any manner whatsoever without written permission except in the case of brief quotations embodied in critical articles or reviews.

This book is a work of fiction. Names, characters, businesses, organizations, places, events and incidents either are the product of the author's imagination or are used fictitiously. Any resemblance to actual persons, living or dead, events, or locales is entirely coincidental.

Book and Cover design by Elizabeth Dickhut

ISBN: 9781549978128

First Edition: November 2024

Credits :

Wendell Berry, "The Peace of Wild Things" from New Collected Poems. Copyright ©2012 by Wendell Berry. Reprinted with the permission of The Permissions Company, LLC on behalf of Counterpoint Press, counterpointpress.com.

Robert Frost, "Going for Water" from *A Boy's Will*, Henry Holt and Company, 1913.

Norman Maclean, *A River Runs through It and Other Stories*, 25th Anniversary Edition. Copyright ©1976 by The University of Chicago Press. Excerpt reprinted with the permission of the Maclean Estate.

AUTHOR'S NOTE

This story was inspired, in part, by my experiences as a high school English teacher. Over my 26 years as a public school teacher, I have witnessed far too many students lose a loved one. Whether it was the loss of a parent, a friend, or a beloved mentor, many of my students grieved in silence, unsure of how to navigate the deep, churning waters of grief.

Some of the students I have taught may feel like they recognize themselves in this story. I assure you, though, that this is a work of fiction. Parker Warren, our grieving boy, represents *many* of my students who have experienced similar pain and loss as well as the hope that sometimes rises to the surface just when they need it most.

For my students

PROLOGUE

"*In medias res*, Parker. That's where the best stories begin." It was advice my father was fond of giving. A lot. I'd even heard him lecture about it to his students on more than one occasion. There he'd be, standing at his podium in front of a roomful of college students, preaching at them about how to write a story while I sat in the back, mapping out my own epic tales with stale crayons and paper I'd swiped from his office.

"*In medias res*. It's Latin for 'in the middle of things,'" he'd tell them, wiggling his fingers in the air, which was his way of saying, *You should write that down*. "That's where you'll start your story. Right in the thick of it." Then he'd steal a glance at me and wink.

But now, at seventeen years old, I never imagined that the timeline of my own life would be marked by such a huge, black dot; and I'm scared as hell to think that my father's death just might be my *in medias res*, like every moment in my life will now fall under one of two categories: Before or After.

Turns out, though, the After isn't at all what I expected.

CHAPTER 1

The Black Dot

"God, this ref *sucks*!" yelled Dante, kicking his soccer ball across the room.

We were all sitting in his basement rewatching what was supposed to be some huge soccer game between Italy and Spain. Turns out, the only real entertainment was watching Dante lose his shit. Repeatedly. "Seriously. This ref sucks ass," he said, throwing himself into a beanbag chair and giving the TV the double salute. "Right?" He was looking at us now, daring us to disagree with him.

"Right," I offered. "He sucks."

"Yeah," agreed Noah, looking at his phone. "Totally. But haven't you already watched this game? You know how it turns out, so why are you still so pissed?"

"Because," Dante hissed, "that's how bad the ref is!"

Gabe and Tony just nodded, and Victor sucked down the rest of his soda before burping a resounding, "*Yuh-Uuurp.*"

"Good one," said Noah.

"Thanks," Victor said, rubbing his chest. "I aim to please."

Honestly, we were all too exhausted — well, all of us except for Dante — to really care about the game. That's because we'd just spent a few hours after school painting some rooms at Borrello's Funeral Home. See, Dante's family owns the funeral home, and his dad had offered us fifty bucks each if we'd do the job. "It needs to be done, and I don't want to spend an arm and a leg," he'd said (which, coming from a funeral director, I thought was a very bad choice of words). The funeral home was built in the 1800s, which really just means that inside there are all sorts of fancy moldings and embellishments, a bunch of stiff antique furniture pushed up against the walls, and crystal chandeliers that catch and throw the light like sparklers. Needless to say, painting a room there is a major pain in the ass. It requires a lot of shuffling around of furniture and standing on a tall, rickety ladder just so you can reach the ceiling.

I remember that Dante had wanted to wait until the weekend to finish the job. "I mean, who's got time in the middle of the week?" he'd argued.

"Dude, we're all free Wednesday after school," I'd argued back. "Besides, what if something happens? What if somebody needs the funeral home? We should just get it done while it's free."

"That's right," Victor said, a giant smirk smeared across his face. "Your dad's stiffies *are* pretty unpredictable."

"And how would you know, Vic?" Noah laughed. "You and Mr. B got something going on that we don't know about? I mean, the least you could do is ask for Dante's blessing first."

"Shut up!" Victor said, a little annoyed. He doesn't like being the dead end of any joke, especially if he's the one who started it.

Maybe I wouldn't have laughed so hard at the stupid joke if I'd known that the next *stiff* would be my father.

It's weird now to think that I played a role in preparing the place for my father's funeral. During the service, I could still smell the fresh paint. I even found myself staring at the spot where my roller had hit the ceiling. It wasn't too noticeable; you'd have to really be looking for it to see it. But for some reason I felt like that little spot was staring back at me, like an evil eye.

To tell you the truth, I was kind of thankful for the mental distraction, even for the paranoid notion that I was being watched by a smudge of paint. Anything to avoid having to look at my dad, or what *resembled* my dad. With all that caked-on makeup and his being stuffed in a suit I don't think I ever saw him wear, he looked more like a cheap wax version of himself.

Anyway, when my mom called me to come home early on what I now refer to as Black Dot Wednesday, I was pissed. "But, Mom," I said, "we're watching the game."

"Park. Parker? Listen to me. You...need to...you need to come home. Now. Right now." Her voice was all shaky, and I could practically feel her panic oozing through the phone.

"I gotta go," I announced to the guys, grabbing my stuff and heading up the stairs.

"Mama's boy!" Victor barked, tossing his crushed can of soda at me.

"Asshole!" I yelled back as I ducked to dodge the can.

When I walked through the backdoor of my house, I slammed it shut with my foot, a move my mom hates. "You aren't mules!" she often shouts at my little brother and me whenever she sees us kicking something open or shut. So there I was, acting like an animal, like a hostile mule, while my mother just stood there in the dark, waiting to tell me the sad, terrible truth.

I remember that a spade of silvery light shot through the window and landed on her face, which was soaked with tears. For the longest time, she couldn't speak. She kept opening and closing her mouth, but nothing came out. Just little shards of noise, broken bits of words that were impossible to piece together.

"Mom?" I said, scared now. "What's wrong?"

"Your dad," she finally managed to say. "He...he died, Parker. He *drowned*," she cried, but she wouldn't — or couldn't — look at us. My brother, Hayden, clung to her, his arms looped around her waist and his head pressed against her shoulder, as if she were the only thing capable of keeping him afloat. "He was...he was kayaking and had...had a heart attack.

Someone found him, but he couldn't.... His kayak...it had flipped over. It...." Her voice just trailed off then, and now she was sobbing again.

I just stood there, my backpack still clinging to my back like a turtle's shell, and I suddenly wished I were small enough to hide inside of it because what she was saying just didn't make any sense.

"No" was all I could say as sour acid climbed up my throat.

My mom finally forced herself to look at me then. "Yes," she whispered back.

And then I threw up all over the kitchen floor.

I got zero sleep that night, not that I even tried. The only thing I could do was stare up at the ceiling and repeat to myself, *This cannot be happening. This cannot be happening. This cannot be happening.* But it was happening, and there was nothing I could do. The only thing I could think to do was go to my mom and my brother, but I was paralyzed. I literally couldn't move, like my own grief had already tied me up and was holding me hostage, demanding an unpayable ransom.

The next morning, when I walked into the kitchen all dressed and slinging my backpack over my shoulder, my mom said, "Where're you going?"

"School," I snapped, like she'd just asked the stupidest question in the world.

"What? Parker, no." She looked past me and scanned the room as if she'd never seen it before. Her eyes were all twitchy and nervous, shifting from side-to-side like on one of those freaky cat clocks. She pinched the top of her robe shut and took a step toward me. "No," she said again. Her chin was trembling, which is what it does when she's trying not to cry. At that moment, though, she didn't look sad. She just looked scared.

"Mom," I said, making an effort to soften the edge of my voice, "I have to go. I can't just...sit around here."

"But what about the...the funeral arrangements? I need your help, Parker. I can't...I can't do this by myself."

"I know. I'll help. I promise. I'll meet you at Borrello's after school." Before she could say anything else, I slipped through the backdoor, refusing the urge to turn around and look at her.

I knew I'd hurt her, leaving her like that. But there was no way in hell that I'd have been able to stare at her wobbling face all day long. There was also the fact that I didn't know how to explain to her that something inside of me had cracked wide open and that I felt like all these emotions had been unleashed, like bats from a cave. There was grief and anger and confusion and denial, all flapping their ugly, black wings. But there was something else, too. A hard, bitter determination. Like all I wanted to do was tell the universe to go fuck itself, and the only way I knew how to do that was to just keep on going.

Away from my house. Away from my mom. Just *away*.

CHAPTER 2

The Mill

Since my mom has barely been able to get out of bed since my dad died, I've been getting up at four o'clock in the morning to open the coffeehouse. See, my mom owns The Mill, the only decent coffeehouse in our little town of Haywood, and I am her most valued (and *overworked*) employee. I have to leave the house before dawn so that I'm at work in time for the bakery delivery. The baker, Nils, is actually only a few years older than I am — I don't think he's even twenty-one yet — but he already has his own catering business. I'm pretty sure he studied culinary arts in high school, but he didn't do much after that. Nothing formal, anyway. No white chef jacket kind of stuff. No collection of fancy knives locked away in a metal case. Still, I think his food is good, and so do our customers.

We opened the coffeehouse when I was still in elementary school, and I've kind of worked there ever since, doing everything from greeting people at the door to bussing tables to manning the register to — finally! — making coffee. My mom, you should know, is *obsessive* about coffee and believes that making it is an art not to be taken lightly. She tastes coffee like some people taste wine, doing the whole swish-it-around-in-your-mouth thing and then spitting it back out into tiny paper cups. Seriously, listening to her talk about the aroma and body of a cup of coffee is kind of like sitting through a goddamn SAT prep class. I mean, who uses words like piquant or alliaceous or leguminous to describe a simple cup of coffee?

I used to roll my eyes, listening to her drone on and on about the finer points of brewing.

Now, she says next to nothing. I don't think I've heard her string together more than three or four words in the last couple of months, not since she had to actually talk to people at the funeral. If she does speak, it's usually to tell me to take care of Hayden because he's too young to take care of himself and because she's too busy wandering around the house in her blue robe and Frankie Say Relax T-shirt, her eyes all bloodshot and puffy and her cheeks red and swollen and riddled with tiny broken capillaries. She looks as if someone marked her face with a red pen in a cruel attempt to point out all of her flaws.

It's freaking Hayden out so much that he's set up camp in my parents' bedroom. About a week ago, I caught him dragging his comforter, a couple of pillows, and a favorite stuffed animal (a teddy bear named Lincoln that I haven't seen in years) into their room.

I stepped on the tail of the comforter when he walked past me and said, "What're you up to, brotato chip?"

He yanked his comforter out from under my foot, which almost made me fall over. "I'm staying with Mom," he said, and I swear he had the look of a general on his face, like he was going to battle or something.

I stood in the hallway, watching. He folded his blankets in the far corner of their room and propped Lincoln up on one of his pillows, and then he took another stuffed animal I hadn't seen — a rabbit, I think — and placed it on my mom's pillow. I looked at him and then just rolled my eyes. I'd be lying, though, if I didn't admit that I'd looked in my room later that day to see if he'd left something for me.

He didn't.

The Mill is only a few blocks from our house, so I always walk, even on dark mornings like this one when the sun hasn't clocked in for its shift yet. I kind of like Haywood best in the morning, when everything still feels a little groggy. I like watching the delivery trucks squeeze into alleyways, their tailgates yawning open. I even like seeing the street lamps flicker until they finally blink off one by one. It's peaceful, this time of day. It's almost enough to trick me into believing that hope is still a thing that hangs in the horizon.

I unlock the door to the coffeehouse and shuffle in, leaving the house lights off because I don't want any early birds knocking before we're open, which they almost always do if

I've turned on the lights. They assume that if the lights are on, then we must be open, even if the sign that's staring them in the face clearly shouts, CLOSED.

The coffeehouse is called The Mill because that's what it used to be: an actual grain mill where they once ground and processed wheat and rye and corn by the ton. Because my mom has a thing for history, she named it for what it once was, not for what it is now. This fascination for all things old is evident everywhere in the coffeehouse. I mean, except for the actual coffee-making stuff (and the art on the walls that changes when some aspiring artist floats in and asks for a favor), everything here was purchased at a flea market, found on the side of the road, or salvaged from some junkyard. The counter near the front windows is a twenty-foot long metal sign that used to hang in a diner; in the middle, making kind of an aisle between the counter and the rest of the tables is an old church pew; and filling every last nook of space are mismatched tables and chairs of varying heights and, admittedly, comfort. Even the lights are an odd collection of pendants and chandeliers that cast a strange glow.

Behind the counter, the first thing I do is turn on the music, loud. Mom is a stickler about the volume; she's even put a piece of masking tape over anything past volume five with *NO!* written on it, as if that's enough to stop me. What can I say? I *need* loud music right now because it prevents my mind from wandering into Dangerous Territory, a place where memories feel more like landmines.

It's not that I don't want to think about my dad. I do. But memories of him don't offer up any kind of consolation;

instead, they're just sad reminders of what I don't have anymore — or, worse — what I'll never have again. Picturing us fishing or remembering a story he told or even thinking about us just reading on the porch, it's like pouring a shit-ton of salt into my very open wound.

With the music almost blaring, I empty a bag of coffee beans into Bonnie, our pet name for the coffee grinder, and start her up. Amazingly, despite all the noise, I hear someone banging around in the kitchen. *Nils,* I think.

There is a loud clattering of metal punctuated by several shouts of "Shit, shit, shit! Goddamn piece of shit!" I'm not sure what he's doing back there, but I'm not too concerned. Nils is one of those people who is just loud. He really has no sense of grace whatsoever, as if he's still getting used to his long, gangly limbs. See, Nils is incredibly tall, nearly seven feet; but he also has a protruding gut, a sort of wide, flat nose, and a very long neck with a freakishly large Adam's apple. To be honest, he's always reminded me of an emu. He sort of has the same ornery temperament, too.

"Morning," he says, carrying a tower of white bakery boxes. He hasn't combed his hair, which is sticking up in every direction, and I catch a strong whiff of morning breath as he passes me on the way to the glass display case.

"Hey," I say. I step out of his way and let him do his thing. He is very particular about how "his work" (his phrase, not mine) is displayed. Scones are expertly piled at just the right angles; muffins are lined up at attention; cinnamon rolls lean against each other, their tight spirals ready to hypnotize customers into buying them. Today, he's also brought some cakes: carrot, chocolate, chocolate-peanut butter, and red velvet. He's already sliced them and squeezed little wax paper sheets between each perfectly proportioned wedge. When he's done, he scoots around to the front of the case to check how they look from a customer's point of view. "Looks good," he mumbles to himself.

"Thanks, Nils," I say, expecting him to go.

He pulls up his sagging pants — his sagging *pajama* pants, I might add — and says, "Did you see that guy in the parking lot when you came in?"

"What guy?"

"There was a guy — old dude, I think — just sitting in his car. Looked like he was watching you." He steps to the window, cups his hands to it, and then peers through them as if he's looking through a pair of binoculars. "Huh," he utters, shrugging. "Whoever he is, he's gone now."

"Are you trying to tell me that I have a stalker? Guess these skinny jeans really do show off my ass," I say, assuming that he's just messing with me. *Hoping* that he is, anyway.

"Hey," he says, setting one hand on a bakery box and raising the other to the ceiling, like he's about to take an oath on a box of muffins. "I wouldn't lie to you about something like that. I take the subject of stalking very seriously."

I feel my eyes stretch to the size of saucers. "Ohhh-kayyy," I manage to say. And now all I can do is imagine him sitting in his van, gnawing on a muffin while he watches some unsuspecting girl through her window.

"Well," I say, glancing at the door, "I've gotta get things going here, so...."

Nils, who evidently can't catch a clue, just stands there. "I'll call later to see if you guys need anything else."

"Okay," I say, looking at the door again.

He's fidgeting now, playing with his keys, looking around the coffeehouse, as if whatever it is he wants to say might suddenly appear on the walls. Finally, he says, "You know, Parker, if you ever...if you need anything, just — "

"Thanks," I interrupt him. "I will." But we both know I won't.

He looks at me for a few seconds more and then nods his head once before heading out through the back of the coffeehouse, his interrupted offer of help hanging in the air.

When he's gone, I look out the window, but no one's there. Just some fog rubbing its back against the pane, leaving behind a skin of dew.

CHAPTER 3

Dudes with Dead Dads

The rest of the day drags its feet, the way it normally does on a Friday when all you really want to do is get the hell out of school and hang out with your friends. On Friday nights, we usually hang out at Gabe and Tony's house, and tonight is no exception. Gabe and Tony are identical twins, but they aren't so identical that you can't tell them apart. Gabe keeps his hair buzzed and has a birthmark the shape of Maine on his neck while Tony wears his hair longer with a big, sweeping wave across the front. Tony is also the louder of the two, but that's not really saying much. They are both incredibly quiet, it's just that Gabe has turned silence into an art, especially at school. He's smart and gets good grades, but he barely says a word. If a teacher puts him on the spot and forces him to answer a question, he kind of closes in on himself, like a hermit crab.

But he wasn't always this way. In fact, he used to be a pretty crazy kid. They both were. The quintessential class clowns, wild and loud and always good for a stupid joke.

That is, until the end of sixth grade.

That's when their dad died. He was on a bus with some other guys heading to work when one of those big box trucks blew a stop sign and hit them. It was big news then because the driver of the box truck was drunk, and the guys on the bus were migrants from Mexico, including Gabe and Tony's dad. A lot of people in town, including my parents, were really upset about the whole thing. I mean, who wouldn't be? So, a bunch of people helped raise some money for the families, and that's when the Rodriguez family (what was left of it) moved into town permanently, out of their trailer near the edge of Tanner's Farm and closer to us.

Back then, when we were eleven years old, how someone died didn't really matter, though. What mattered was that the person was just gone. Come to think of it, it still really doesn't matter because the end result is the same.

That was only two years before Noah's dad died of brain cancer. I remember that Noah missed a lot of school then. He was with his father when he died. He got to say goodbye at least.

So I guess you could say that we've formed a kind of de facto club for Dudes with Dead Dads. We should make it official. Start our own blog or something. I mean, even Dante, whose dad is obviously not dead, would still qualify because his dad's business is death. Our fathers' funerals were at Borrello's Funeral Home, after all, so why not make Dante an honorary member?

And Victor? Let's just say that his dad is never around and is, quite honestly, a major douche. So he, too, is an honorary member of the saddest fucking club in the world.

Anyway, it's Friday night, so we (just Gabe, Tony, Dante and I) are hanging out in the shed near the back of Gabe and Tony's yard. The shed is actually meant to store yard equipment, lawnmowers and the like, but we quickly took it over when they first moved in. Back then we used to pretend that the shed was the Death Star, so we'd shoot at it with our Nerf Guns, believing ourselves to be part of the Rebel Alliance. Because Noah was the tallest we'd always make him play Darth Vader. He would complain at first, but he actually loved playing a bad guy. Plus, he was really good at mimicking Vader's heavy breathing.

Now the shed is just where we hang out, especially if there's nothing else really going on, which is often the case since Haywood feels like a blink-and-you'll-miss-it kind of town. We've got posters of our favorite bands plastering most of the walls, white Christmas lights zigzagging the ceiling, an old couch crammed up against the far end, and a small card table perched in the middle with a few dented, mismatched folding chairs snugged up against it. There's an old, broken guitar leaning in the one corner, and a few ashtrays dotting the floor. In the colder months, we use an electric heater, the kind with the coils that glow red, which is probably a serious fire hazard. It's a small price to pay for a space to call our own. Right now, since the weather has finally warmed up and the bugs seem already to be in full force, strips of yellow flypaper hang from the ceiling like stalactites.

Dante passes me a bowl that he's fashioned out of an apple. I shake my head no and he just shrugs, as if to say, *Your loss*.

"Dude, why're you using an apple?" Tony asks, taking the apple/bowl from Dante.

"Because," Dante says, "I'm trying to be healthy."

I laugh. "You are truly a dumbass."

"I'm a genius, actually. Because when I get hungry, I can just eat the apple."

"Gross," Gabe says, his first utterance of the evening.

"Where's Noah?" Tony asks, as he leans his head against the back of the couch and releases a long thread of smoke.

"Probably at Lisa's begging for forgiveness," Dante answers with an eye roll so loud that I'm pretty sure the neighbors heard it. Picture an Italian dude, and Dante'd be it. He's got darker skin and hairy limbs and eyes so brown they're almost black. His black hair is long and extremely curly, so he usually wears it pulled back. I'm pretty sure he keeps it long just to piss off his dad.

"What he do this time?" I ask, not really interested. Noah and Lisa have a love/hate relationship. They've been dating on and off again since middle school and still can't figure out that they just don't fit together, like two pieces from two very different puzzles. It's pretty pointless to try and keep up with their day-to-day drama.

"Apparently, he dared to text some freshman," Dante says, picking at a loose scab on his elbow.

"Who?" I ask.

"Maeve Winters," Dante says, more interested in his elbow, which is now bleeding.

"Can't blame him," I say. "She's pretty hot."

"So what," coughs Tony. "Freshmen girls are too high maintenance. They need, like, constant reminders of your undying love for them. It's exhausting."

"¿Qué sabrías de esto?" asks Gabe, his voice all scratchy and out of tune, probably because this is the first time he's really used it all day.

"Más de lo que sabes, idiota." Tony picks up a bottle cap from the floor and throws it at his brother. Then he says, "Hey, tell Parker what Mom told us."

"Le dices," Gabe says, spinning the cap like a top.

Tony takes another drag and then fights to hold the smoke in his lungs. "Estoy ocupado," he manages to say, his face all tight as if he's in pain, so I know his lungs must be burning.

"In English, *por favor*," I say, getting a little annoyed.

Gabe rolls his eyes. His tolerance for my lack of Spanish skills is nonexistent. "She said that some old guy checked in at the motel yesterday."

The twins' mom manages the Haywood Motel, a rundown, one-story building that sits on a three-corner intersection at the edge of town. And by manage, I mean that she literally does everything there: runs the front desk, cleans the rooms, and does minor repairs. Most importantly, she knows the comings and goings of just about everyone in town.

"And this is breaking news because?" I ask.

"Because," Tony says, breathing again, "he's got the same

last name as you."

"Really?"

"Yep."

"So?"

"Well, you're the only Warrens in town. He's probably related to you."

"Doubt it."

Gabe rubs at his chin, a habit he's picked up since he's finally managed to grow what looks like the ghost of a beard. "She said that he asked about your mom."

This gets my attention. "Really? What'd he want?"

"We don't know," Tony says. "Mom said she didn't want to 'entertain the conversation.' Whatever the hell that means."

Dante slaps my shoulder with the back of his hand. "I wouldn't worry about it, bro. It's probably nothing."

"Yeah," I say. "Right." I'm wondering if I should mention what Nils told me this morning, about an old man watching me through the window, but I decide to keep quiet about it because I don't want to even try and connect these dots.

CHAPTER 4

Monday, Monday (Part One)

On Monday morning I'm stuck at the coffeehouse later than usual because Madge, one of our baristas, is late.

Hey, don't let the old lady name fool you. Madge is only twenty-five, and she still lives with her parents. She claims that she "has a plan," but I have no idea what it is. I'd bet a fortune that it has something to do with reading or writing since she always has a book hidden under the counter and devours a few pages when she thinks nobody's looking, which, if you saw Madge, you'd soon realize that *everyone* is looking at her. She is what my dad would refer to as "fairy tale beautiful." She's got long, thick blond hair and blue eyes with flecks of gold, and her skin just seems to glow. Seriously. It's like someone's dusted every inch of her with crushed diamonds. This is why it really doesn't help that most of her books look as if they've been dropped in the bathtub. Whenever I catch her reading, all I can do is picture her lounging in the tub.

Madge also has a habit of scribbling down random thoughts on napkins or wasted receipts and then stuffing them into her pockets. Basically, I think her mind is a tangled mess of words, and if she doesn't tease some of them out every once in a while, they'll get even more knotted up inside of her pretty head.

It's this obsession with words that got her hired in the first place. See, Madge is what Mom considers "one of Dad's projects." He had a habit of offering jobs at the coffeehouse to his more promising writing students because in his mind, coffeehouses are natural habitats for writers. That, or he just liked filling his spaces with likeminded people. Then again, who doesn't?

I will say this about Madge, though: She is absolutely focused at work when she's making coffee, especially espressos, lattes, and cappuccinos. As it turns out, nobody does foam like Madge. "She's an artist," Mom always says. I agree. Madge *is* an artist. I just happen to think that she'd rather work with words than with foam.

"Sorry," she says as she rushes through the door. Her cheeks are flushed and her hair untamed, as if she's just flown in from some enchanted forest.

"It's okay," I say, despite the fact that Madge has given me exactly ten minutes to complete what's normally a twenty-minute walk to school.

"No, really. I'm sorry. I fell asleep reading last night and forgot to set the alarm." She's already behind the counter tying on an apron. "Shoo," she tells me, giving me a little shove toward the door.

When I get to school, I head straight to English class instead of going to my locker first. Dante's already there, finishing an assignment that's due today. "Hey," I say, sliding into the seat next to him.

"Hey," he says back without looking up, his pen skating across the page.

Noah walks in just before the last bell rings, which is pretty typical. Mrs. Daniels is still out in the hall talking with some other teachers, so it's safe to say that we have a few minutes before class is really going to start. When Noah sits down, Dante closes his notebook and says, "What'd you do all weekend? Hang out with Lisa?"

"Nah, that's a negative. I had to resort to plan B," Noah says, digging into his bag for his notebook.

"Oh," Dante nods. "So what you're saying is that you just played video games and jerked off all weekend?"

"Pretty much," Noah says, smiling.

Sarah, who sits in front of Noah, turns around and says, "You guys are so gross." She says the word *gross* so that it sounds like two syllables instead of one.

"Oh, like you don't," Noah says, giving her a friendly shove in the back.

"What? Jerk off?" Sarah says, both annoyed and entertained. "I think not."

"Maybe not yourself," Dante says with a smirk, "but probably Victor."

Sarah's cheeks turn red, but she still laughs. "Shut the

hell up, Dante!"

We're all laughing now. We always give Sarah a hard time for hooking up with Victor, but it's only because we like Sarah. Victor is our friend, but even we can admit that he can be a real asshole, especially to girls. If you ask me, Sarah could do a lot better than Victor.

When Sarah turns around to face the front of the room, we lock eyes, briefly. At my dad's funeral, when they lowered him into the ground, Sarah held my hand. I don't remember too much about that day, but I do remember that. I also remember that it was cold. And windy. It was one of those early spring days that looks and feels more like winter. But Sarah's fingers were woven with my own, and in that moment, it was enough to keep me a little warm. Since then I've wondered what it might be like to hold her hand again, on an ordinary day.

Mrs. Daniels finally makes her way into the classroom. "Good morning, everyone!" she says in a voice that's way too cheerful for a Monday morning. However, we are quickly approaching the final month of school, so all of the teachers have a little extra spring in their steps. I suspect that they like summer vacation just as much as we do. Maybe more.

"So," Mrs. Daniels says, taking a sip of coffee from a mug that proudly proclaims, THIS ISN'T COFFEE. Mrs. Daniels has an odd sense of humor. That, or she's secretly a raging alcoholic. She picks up a big stack of papers and says, "I present your review packets, my friends."

Shit. Review, I think. I really hate review season at school. It's boring as hell. It makes me want to seriously slap

Gavin the Stoner, who's sitting next to me. How this guy landed in an Honors English class is beyond me. The kid barely comes to school; and when he does, it's only after he's smoked a joint in the patch of woods between the school and the bowling alley. At this point, he's incapable of using consonant sounds at the ends of words. If a teacher asks him a question, his response is usually "Whah?" or "Huh?" So, essentially, this review is for him; however, he's so stoned out of his mind that I doubt he'll remember anything that Mrs. Daniels says. She should save herself the headache and give him a failing grade now.

The rest of the day limps along as usual. Trig, then APUSH, then gym, then lunch; AP Bio, study hall, Sports Marketing, and then Accounting. Most of it just more review. At some point during Accounting, I get a text from Madge. She's supposed to stay at the coffeehouse until 5:00, but she's not feeling well and wondering if I would come in after school to cover the rest of her shift. I consider telling her that she should go home and take a hot bath, but I don't. Instead, I just text OK, happy to go to her rescue.

When I get to the coffeehouse, Madge unties her apron and hands it to me. "Your mom's in back," she says, grabbing her book from under the counter. I can't help but notice the little beads of sweat on her forehead. God, she even makes sweat look good.

"She's here?" I ask, surprised. And relieved. I was beginning to worry that my mom would never leave the house again.

"Yeah. She came in this morning."

"Really? That's good."

Madge runs her thumb along the edge of her book. Her eyes sneak past me and move toward the back of the coffeehouse as she says, "Your mom. She's...."

"She's what?" I ask, a little worried now.

"Never mind," Madge says. "Just...be happy she's here. And be nice." She points a warning finger at me before she turns to leave.

Before I take my post behind the counter, I straighten up some papers on the tables near the front of the coffeehouse. There's always a lazy customer who leaves his dishes around, so I pick those up, too. It's best to get ahead of the mess before things really get busy. The after-school crowd (which, believe it or not, is my least favorite collection of customers) will be showing up soon for their frozen coffees and smoothies, and they definitely leave their garbage everywhere but the actual trash can.

When I'm done cleaning up a bit, my mom emerges from the back, like a moth from its cocoon, with a clipboard and pen in hand. "Hi, Parker," she says as she starts counting bags of coffee, pointing at each one with her pen.

"Hey, Mom!" I say, my voice cracking under the pressure of fake cheerdom.

"How was school?" she asks, but she doesn't look at me.

"Fine. Just review mostly."

"Well, that's good," she says, setting her clipboard down and recording a number.

Knowing that she absolutely hates taking inventory, I

offer to take over. "Mom, you want me to do that? I don't mind. Really."

"No. That's okay."

"Are you sure? Because — "

"Parker!" she snaps, slamming the clipboard down and shaking all over. "I said it's fine. Please. Just let me do it."

"Okay. *Sorry*," I say, turning on Bonnie, needing some noise.

My mom doesn't say anything else for a few minutes. She goes back to counting bags of coffee, nearly stabbing them with the business end of her pen. It's then that I notice she's wearing slippers. *Slippers!* I'm not sure if she didn't remember to change into shoes or if she just didn't care. I almost say something to her, but then I remember what Madge said about just being happy that she's here. So, I try to ignore the slippers and to focus instead on the fact that she's not wearing her robe, too.

"Parker," she sighs, hugging the clipboard to her chest. "Can you just...man the front of the house? I have to go pick up your brother."

"Sure. No problem."

She looks at me for a moment and then jerks her head away, as if it pains her to look at me for too long. It probably does. I am, after all, the spitting image of my father. I have a mess of brown hair with the same stubborn cowlick; I have his mossy green eyes; and I have his dimpled chin. Hell, I even have his height, too. I'd finally been able to look him square in the eye without standing on my toes just before he died.

So, yeah, my mom must really hate looking at me.

"Oh, I forgot," she says, "Charlie's supposed to show up in a little bit, but you should be fine by yourself until he gets here."

"Charlie's home from college already?"

"Yes," she answers as she heads toward the back of the coffeehouse. She turns around, like she's forgotten something, and says, "Love you."

"Love you, too, Mom."

I can hear her slippers scrape against the floor like fine sandpaper. And then out of nowhere, a storm kicks up in my head, flinging memories every which way. First I'm thinking of my dad tucked away in that box, and then I see the stunned, deer-in-headlights look on my mom's face when they lowered him into the ground. I even see the black hat she wore, not because she's formal like that, but because Dad always liked her in hats.

And then I remember something from Before: Dad bought her those slippers for her birthday, just two weeks before he died.

CHAPTER 5

Monday, Monday (Part Two)

When Charlie walks in, he looks different. I'd say more confident, but he's always been confident. I guess I'd say that he just looks more like *himself*. His jeans are rolled up to just above his ankles, and his polo shirt is buttoned all the way up. His hair is buzzed, except for the top, which is long and slicked back. He also has a beard. And a tattoo on his left forearm. I'll just admit it right now: Charlie is kind of my idol. He's just always been the epitome of cool.

"Parker!" he says, as if announcing my presence to the entire world. "What's up, man?" He shakes my hand and then leans in for a brief hug. Charlie is the son of my dad's best friend, Leo, so I've pretty much known him forever. The last time I saw him, though, was at my dad's funeral. Actually, he was there for *all* of it. The calling hours (both sets), the funeral, the luncheon at The Mill. Charlie loved my dad and often referred to him as Uncle Jack. That's how close our families are. Charlie wept at my dad's funeral, and I mean *real* weeping. The chest-choking, snot-all-over-your-face kind of weeping.

But I haven't cried yet.

When my mom told me what happened, the mechanisms in my body went all haywire. My ears filled with fluid; my knees buckled beneath me so that I could hardly stand, let alone walk; and then my stomach turned to acid. And then, like I told you before, I threw up. But I didn't cry. It's not that my dad doesn't deserve my tears. He does. He deserves a lakeful of tears. It's just...I don't know. I'm beginning to think there's something wrong with me, like I need a serious recalibration in the Emotions Department.

Charlie grabs an apron from the back and ties it around his waist. "How's your mom?" he asks. One thing you can always count on with Charlie is that he's not one for small talk. He steps right over the bullshit and skips to the important stuff.

"Not great. But she was here today, so I guess that's something."

"Yeah. It is. And what about you and Hay?"

"I don't know." This is true. I don't really know how Hayden is, but I'd guess that he probably feels like I do, somewhere between surviving and wanting to jump off a bridge.

Charlie crosses his arms and leans against the counter. "My dad's opening the meadery next weekend. You should come." The meadery was a project that my dad and Leo had been working on together for years. It all started as my dad's idea. Well, honestly, it was kind of one of his student's ideas. See, every spring he taught a class on epic poetry; and one day, while discussing the importance of the mead hall in *Beowulf* (a terribly boring Anglo-Saxon epic, by the way), a student said, "We need a mead hall in Haywood. I hate beer, but fermented honey sounds delicious." And that's all it took. That night my dad was on the phone with Leo developing plans for their own mead hall, which they decided to call The Beehive.

"I don't know," I finally say. "Maybe." Truth is, I really don't want to go.

"C'mon," he says, slapping my shoulder. "We'll help ourselves to some samples. They've got this one called Bee Spit. It's great."

"Bee Spit? Sounds...appetizing."

Charlie laughs in agreement. "I know, right? But it's actually really good."

"Who came up with that name?" I ask, fairly certain I already know the answer.

"Yours truly," he says, taking a bow.

I laugh. "Good thing you're not a marketing major. You'd be failing miserably."

Charlie, pretending to be offended, says, "Hey, as long as it tastes good, it doesn't matter what they call it."

"I guess."

The after-school crowd comes and goes. It's hot out, one of the first truly hot days in May, so we make more smoothies than anything else, which means the industrial blender is running nonstop. "Enough with the damn smoothies," Charlie laments, rubbing his temples. I agree. The perpetual whir of the blender is enough to give you a pounding headache.

When it's almost five o'clock, an old man — someone I know I've never seen before but who also looks strangely familiar — shuffles into the coffeehouse. He walks slowly to the counter and looks straight at me, like he knows me. I can tell he wants to say something, that he's kind of struggling for some words, because he keeps opening and closing his mouth, like a distressed fish mouthing the surface of the water. *Maybe he's got Alzheimer's,* I think, recalling an elderly woman who'd walked in here one day and asked for her dry cleaning.

"Can I help you?" I ask, trying to help the poor man along.

He doesn't respond. He just stares at me, like he's studying my face. It's so intense, his stare, that I have to look away. Thankfully, his eyes scoot past me and move around the coffeehouse.

I try again. "Sir?" I say, louder this time. "Can I help you?"

"Is...Grace Warren here?" he finally asks, his eyes landing on me again, heavy as stone.

Holy shit, I think, getting a little freaked out now because I'm wondering if this is the old man Gabe and Tony were telling me about. The same old man who was watching me through the window the other day.

"Uh, no. Sorry. She's not here," I manage to say, "but I can take a message if you want." I reach for a pen and a pad of paper, but the old man has already started toward the door.

"No," he says. "No message." He walks out of the shop, and I watch him as he goes. Outside, he just stands on the sidewalk, looking up and down the street as if deciding which way to go. He pulls a piece of paper from his pocket and studies it before he heads north, toward my part of town.

"That was so weird, dude," Charlie says as he helps himself to a cup of coffee. "Like, *really* weird."

I nod. "Yeah. I know. I think he's probably just lost or confused or something." But even I can hear the uncertainty in my voice.

"That's not what I mean."

"No? What do you mean then?"

Charlie shakes his head, slowly. "That guy could have been your dad, like thirty years from now."

"Nah," I say, swatting at the air, treating Charlie's comment as if it were nothing more than a pesky gnat. But he's right. The man *did* look like my dad. The dad that I'll never see. The Future Dad. The Old Man Dad.

CHAPTER 6

Connecting the Dots

For dinner, Mom pulls another casserole from the freezer. After Dad died, people kept dropping off food. Cookies and cakes and casseroles mostly. All stuff we don't normally eat, but since Mom doesn't feel like cooking and it's too convenient, we've had a casserole every night since the funeral. Tonight, it's shepherd's pie.

We eat in silence. Our forks tapping and scraping against our plates, like some sorry-ass SOS signal. Hayden has spent most of dinner pushing his vegetables to the edge of his plate, creating a circle of mushy, dimpled peas and brown carrots. I'm waiting for him to flick one of the peas at me with his finger. The old Hayden would have; this Hayden doesn't. This Hayden is wearing one of Dad's old sweatshirts. The same one he's been wearing for about a week. The cuffs are damp and frayed because he's been chewing on them, a habit from back when he was toddler, and one that he'd outgrown. Or so I thought.

My mom hasn't touched much of her dinner, either, but she has managed to finish a couple glasses of wine.

I'm just trying not to look at Dad's chair, but the more I try *not* to look at it, the more it wants to be seen.

When someone you love dies, his absence is *felt*. It becomes its own thing. It glares at you. It dares you to ignore it, but it's impossible to ignore because it has a loud, deafening silence that simply demands to be heard.

"This sucks," Hayden declares, tossing his fork on the table.

"Yes," Mom agrees. The dinner, the silence, everything. All of it sucks.

"Pizza?" Mom asks, a small lift to her voice.

"Yes!" we yell in desperate unison.

Hayden, with more enthusiasm than he's exhibited in weeks, jumps up from his chair and takes his plate to the sink. He even clears our plates, including the casserole dish. He happily scrapes what's left of the shepherd's pie into the sink and flips on the garbage disposal. The disposal chomps and chews on the remains of the casserole and then ends with what can only be described as a very long, satisfied belch. "Well," Hayden says, "at least *somebody* likes it."

Then a miracle happens: Mom laughs.

Hayden and I both swing around to look at her. She seems surprised, too, because her hand is covering her mouth and her eyes are stretched wide open. I wonder if she's ashamed that she dared to think that something was funny, as if laughing too soon might in some way betray Dad.

In an attempt to reassure her that she's done nothing wrong, I say, "Good one, Hay." And then I hold my breath because I don't know what to do next, and I don't know what Mom is going to do, either. I'm afraid that she might shut herself in her room again, close herself off from us. She used to be so generous with her laughter, even though it's not a pretty laugh. Like, she's got one of those laughs that sounds more like a honk than a trill. That's why Dad always called her The Goose.

Much to my relief — and I'm sure Hayden's as well — she smiles. Another miracle.

You know how on a cloudy day, when the wind is sharp and bitter, and then suddenly there's a break in the clouds and there's sunlight spilling all over the ground? That's what her smile felt like just then. It was like the clouds parting and the sun suddenly warming us. As lame as that sounds, there's really no other way to describe it.

Later, after we've stuffed ourselves with pizza, Hayden goes up to his room to play video games. Mom actually tells him that he's only allowed to play for half an hour. *Finally*, I think, *she's back to Mom Mode.*

I sit down at the kitchen table to do some math review while Mom loads the dishwasher, and it's now that I remember about the old man. Actually, to tell you the truth, he's sort of been on my mind the entire evening, in and out of focus like a flickering film. I keep seeing his craggy, yet familiar face. His determined, searching stare.

"Mom?" I say.

"Yeah?" she says as she slams the dishwasher shut with her hip.

"Some old guy was in the coffee shop today asking for you." I pretend to focus on a math problem.

"Oh, yeah? Who was it?" she asks, pouring herself another glass of wine. A bigger one this time.

"Don't know. He sort of walked out when I asked him if he wanted to leave you a message."

Mom sips her wine, stares out the window. "Oh, well. I guess he'll come back if it's important enough."

"I guess," I say. I try to work out a complicated equation, but I can't concentrate because Charlie's words keep circling in my head, like beady-eyed crows. "Charlie said something kinda weird about the guy."

"What's that?"

I'm not sure where to go from here. I want to tell her to forget it, but Mom is not one to let a story hang around unfinished. Once you've started to tell her something, she won't let you go in reverse. It only makes her suspicious. So I keep going, despite the risk it poses. For both of us. "He said...that the guy could be Dad. Thirty years from now." Quickly, to fill the silence that threatens to build around us, I lie and say, "But I didn't think so."

Mom puts her wine glass down and steadies herself on the edge of the counter, hunching over as if she's been struck with some sharp, terrible pain. "Oh, my God," she whispers to herself. She spins around, heads to the front of the house, and comes back with an envelope clutched in her hands. I can see that there's no address on it, just her name scrawled across the front in black ink.

"What's that?" I ask. I'm two parts worried and one part curious.

"This was in the door when I got home, but I just threw it in with the rest of the mail." Her hands are shaking as she rips it open. Slowly, she pulls out a handwritten note. I get up to read it, too. I'm plenty tall enough to read over her shoulder.

> Dear Grace,
> I know that it's been many years. Too many I'd care to admit to. But I got Jackie's letter a while back, and I've only now worked up the nerve to face him. I guess I waited too long. For that – and for many other things – I am sorry.
> I would like to speak with you, though. I'm staying at the Haywood Motel. I don't have a cell phone, so you can just call there. That is, if you want to.
> John Warren

"What the hell?" I say, snatching the letter from her hand, reading it again.

"Unbelievable," she says with an almost-smile on her face.

"Is this who I think it is?"

Then she really does smile. "Yeah, Parker. It's your grandfather."

CHAPTER 7

Plot Twist

My dad's father walked out on his family when my dad was seventeen, the same age I am now.

When I was younger, maybe five or six, it suddenly dawned on me that my dad didn't have a dad. I remember we were watching *Star Wars*, and it was during that scene in *Episode V*, the one where Vader tells Luke he's his father, when I turned to my dad and said, "Who's your dad?"

"Who's *my* dad?" he asked, a little surprised.

"Yeah. Who is he?"

"Darth Vader."

I laughed. "No, no, no."

"Uh...Chewbacca," he said, tickling my feet and grunting like Chewie.

I hid my feet between the sofa's cushions and said again, "C'mon, Dad. Who?"

He got all serious then and pulled me closer to him. "His name is John."

"Where is he?" I wanted to know. "How come I've never seen 'im?"

"Well," he said, "he went on a trip and didn't come back."

"Why not? Did he die?"

"No. He just...wasn't happy. And sometimes when people aren't happy, they leave."

"But *you're* happy."

I must've looked worried or something because he hugged me and said, "Don't worry, kiddo. I'm not going anywhere."

There were other times over the years when I asked my dad about his father, about why his old man left. Nearly every time my dad would say the same thing: "My father was unhappy, and that's about all I know." But there was something about how he'd said it — the sudden dip in his voice, the need to look away — that always made me think that he was hiding something from me.

I remember that right after my dad died, I wondered how he must have felt, losing his dad when he did. How he handled it. If he ever cried when he finally realized that his father wasn't coming back. Then I thought, *But his dad didn't die. He just left!* Maybe that's worse, though, being left by choice. After all, my dad was *taken* from us. If he'd been given the choice, he'd be here right now, standing in this kitchen, reading this letter, knowing what to do.

"Your dad wanted to find him," my mom starts to explain, but

I can't really hear her because I'm getting that same feeling that I had when she told me that Dad was gone. Her words sound as if they're traveling through water, and I kind of feel like I'm going to throw up.

"But why would Dad *want* to find him?" I yell, mostly because I can barely hear myself.

Mom reaches up and cups my chin in her hand. "I know it's hard to understand. That it doesn't make much sense. But your dad, he...he just needed to find him, to talk to him. Honestly — " she stops herself, fiddles with her necklace. It's one of those necklaces with our birthstones on it, something we bought for her a couple of years ago for Mother's Day. I notice now that she's added Dad's wedding ring to it, and it's the ring that she's moving back and forth on the chain.

"Honestly *what*?" I say, moving my jaw around, trying to free the fluid from my ears.

She sighs and then folds her arms across her chest. "I think your turning seventeen had something to do with it. It churned up a bunch of feelings for him."

"Great. So it's my fault," I say, slumping back into my chair and pushing my notebook across the table.

My mom, who's not one to tolerate open displays of self-pity, says, "Parker, stop it. You know that's not what I mean."

"Sorry," I growl. "Still. His timing sucks."

"Agreed."

We sit for a few minutes, neither of us saying anything. It's an unexpected twist in a plot that we're still getting used to, and I can't help but get angry with my dad all over again because not only did he have the nerve the die, but he still gets to be the author of our story, taking us on a detour that I sure as hell don't want to take.

I ask a question that I pretty much already know the answer to: "So you knew that Dad was looking for him?"

"Yes, of course. But...then...." She can't go on. She's about to cry. Her left hand leaps up to touch Dad's ring again.

"Yeah. I know."

Mom sits down next to me. She reaches over and squeezes my hand. I squeeze back.

"So what're you going to do?" I ask.

"Well, I guess I'll go over to the motel tomorrow."

"And what about Hayden? Are you going to tell him?"

"Yes. I suppose I should. I don't want him taken off guard like you were. I don't think he could handle it."

"Agreed," I say.

She kisses the top of my head and then goes upstairs, presumably to tell Hayden. I think about going with her, but then I don't. Instead, I wait until she's all the way upstairs and then gulp down the rest of her wine. It leaves my tongue feeling sort of dry and puckery. I'm not sure if this is a good thing, but I don't like it. I don't like it one bit.

CHAPTER 8

Waiting (Im)Patiently

At school, it's next to impossible to focus. I keep imagining what my mom's encounter with the old man will be like. I try to imagine the words they might say, the gestures they might make, but imagining is difficult when you can only predict one side of the conversation. I can guess — I think with a fair amount of certainty — at what my mom might say, but I have no idea what kind of words might tumble out of the old man's mouth.

In my opinion, he'd better damn well start with an avalanche of *I'm sorrys*.

I'm not usually one to have my phone out too much during class. Today, though, I find myself slipping my phone from my pocket every ten seconds.

Anyway, it's already third period, and no update

whatsoever from my mom.

In APUSH, it's especially difficult to concentrate. Mr. Lawton isn't at his usual post behind his podium. Instead, he is sitting at a student desk, facing us, which means that we have a clear, unhindered view of his feet. His *sandaled* feet. See, Mr. Lawton wears sandals year round, even when it's freezing outside. He has to. The second toe on his right foot is permanently bent at a ninety-degree angle, apparently making it rather difficult to wear regular shoes. At least in the winter, though, he wears socks. But not today. Today, the toe is fully exposed in all of its glory, and it feels like it's staring at me.

When the bell finally rings and we're safely down the hall, Noah says, "God, that toe freaks me out."

Victor, who has Mr. Lawton later in the day, says, "No socks today, I presume?"

"Nope," I say, checking my phone again.

"It's so freaking weird! It's like a periscope," Noah says when we get to his locker. "I swear, it even moves back and forth, like it's spying on you." He moves his head from side-to-side to imitate the infamous toe and its periscopic movement.

The best I can offer is a disinterested smirk. "I know. It's creepy." I check my phone. Again.

"Obsess much?" Victor says to me, plucking my phone from my hand and checking the screen.

"Hey!" I yell, snatching it back.

"Sorry, but you've looked at that thing like a million times today. Is Madge sending you naked pictures of herself or something?" I'm not the only one who thinks Madge is hot.

"I wish." This isn't true. (Of course, it isn't *un*true, either.)

From a distance, we see Sarah walking toward us. Victor slaps me on the back and says, "Gotta go, boys!" before heading down the hall, bobbing and weaving his way through the crowd. No doubt he's trying to avoid her. That's what he generally does in between random hook ups with Sarah. I say random, but there is a certain pattern to them: Whenever Victor calls, Sarah answers. It's never the other way around, which is to say that when Sarah calls Victor, he *never* answers.

My next class, Bio Lab, happens to be with Sarah, so I wait for her. The smile that she was wearing as she walked down the hall has already faded to nothing. No trace of it on her face whatsoever. I'm suddenly overcome with a strong desire to punch Victor in the throat.

"Hey," I say to her, doing my best to offer up a smile of my own.

"Hi," she says, watching Victor make his way through the hall, away from her.

Thankfully, we aren't doing much in AP Bio anymore. We took the AP test a couple of weeks ago, so we're just working on our final project for the rest of the year. Our class is teaming up with one of the tech classes to create a display called The Evolution of Things, which shows how certain species — or, for the tech kids, *inventions* — have evolved over time. The small but vocal Christ Crowd isn't too pleased with Mrs. Reiner's assignment this year, but she doesn't care. She's a scientist. Empirical evidence is her god.

Anyway, Sarah and I are partners for the project. We

decided to show the evolution of birds, proving how they evolved from dinosaurs. Today, we're supposed to put the finishing touches on our papier-mâché pterodactyl. We picked birds because Sarah has a pet parakeet named Tom Cat. (Sarah likes being ironic.) "We'll have a *live* specimen," she'd said when she first suggested that we research birds. She's even trained it to answer "Charles Darwin" when asked who its daddy is. "Shouldn't it at least say 'Terry' for pterodactyl? Or something like that. I mean, isn't that our point here?" I'd argued. To which she responded, "Parker, it's a *joke*."

Joke or not, we are guaranteed to get an A.

The pterodactyl is huge. We made its wingspan at least eight feet across, and its wings are what we need to finish painting today. The painting, for some reason, relaxes me a bit. Or maybe it's Sarah. I don't know. But I haven't checked my phone in a while, so that's something.

"So," Sarah says, concentrating on her brushstrokes, "how are you?"

"Fine," I say.

"Liar."

"No, really," I say, trying to sound more convincing, more upbeat. So much so that my voice practically squeaks. "I'm fine."

"Uh huh." She's bent down, working on the bottom of a wing, so she has to look up at me. I can't see her mouth because it's hidden beneath the wing, but I can tell she's smiling at me because I can see it in her eyes, which almost squint shut when she smiles.

I stop painting. I want to tell her. I want to tell her

about the old man, about how my dad's past has swept into town like a ghost. The words are there, bubbling up inside of me, rising to the surface. I open my mouth. I'm about to tell her when Mrs. Reiner walks up behind me and says, "Good work, Parker and Sarah. Truly excellent effort."

Sarah stands up and rinses her paintbrush in a cup of water. "Thanks, Mrs. Reiner."

"Yeah," I say, "thanks a lot."

CHAPTER 9

The Old Man

When I walk through the back door into the kitchen, I hear muffled voices coming from the living room, which is at the front of the house. Our house is an old Victorian home, with separate, chambered rooms. Noises, therefore, don't travel very well. They get lost snaking their way through endless doorways and hallways until they seem to finally give up and slither away. Still, I can hear people talking. My mom and someone else. A man.

The old man. The supposed grandfather. It has to be. I mean, who else *could* it be?

I am frozen. I am stuck mid-step. I am half-tempted to turn around and run, but then I hear my mom calling me. "Parker?" she yells. "Parker, we're in the living room."

We? I think to myself. *There's already a WE?*

I do not want to go in there. Then, I hear another voice. Hayden's.

My stomach cinches and twists. I feel like someone is trying to wring me out like a rag.

"Par-*ker*!" my mom yells again.

"I'm *coming*!" I call back, sounding all pissed off. I can't help it. I'm angry that my mom's even invited this man into our home, this man who abandoned my dad so many years ago; and I'm angry that they've been here, talking. Without me. Simply put: It's the worst kind of anger. The confused kind, the kind that shoots off in a hundred different directions, like a firecracker.

I pass through the dining room into the foyer and then hesitate before I step into the living room, which is to the left. We hardly ever spend any time here. The furniture, antique stuff that my mom had reupholstered, is stiff and unyielding and practically forces you to sit up straight. Honestly, I think the term *living room* is kind of misleading because there's not much living that takes place in it. Of course, you'd never know that now. My little brother is sitting on the floor, thumbing through a photo album; my mom is perched on the edge of the couch, pointing at a photograph that I can't quite see; and the old man is in the armchair, holding a cup of coffee and straining his neck to see whatever picture it is that my mom has found.

Yes, it's the perfect family tableau. A real Norman Rockwell moment. Except when you consider the fact that the wrong man is sitting where my father should be.

"Hi," I say, unable to utter more than a single syllable.

I'm leaning against the frame of the archway. I haven't actually stepped *into* the living room yet. It's kind of like standing at the edge of a lake for the first time. Best to dip just your toes in first, test the waters.

My mom stands up when she sees me, and I can tell that she's nervous because she doesn't know what to do with her hands. One hand is looking for a pocket to hide in, but the pants she's wearing don't have pockets; and the other hand is playing with her necklace, the one with Dad's ring hanging from it. "Parker," she says, trying to smile, "this is John. John Warren, your — "

"I know who he is," I snap.

Ruddy patches blossom on my mom's face, so I know she's embarrassed. And probably ticked off.

The old man takes a few slow, cautious steps my way, as if he's approaching a strange dog he's not sure he can trust. I don't move to meet him halfway. I can't. The frame of the archway is the only thing holding me up.

When he does get close enough, he reaches his right hand toward me. His fingers are fat; the knuckles swollen. They remind me of the knobs on a tree, spots where the limbs have broken away. "Nice to meet you, Parker," John says, his voice deep and rumbling and foreboding as distant thunder. I stare at his shaking hand. I don't want to touch it, but my mom is watching me, her eyebrows squeezing together and her face ready to wear the dreaded Mask of Disappointment.

So, I shake his hand. And I squeeze it. Hard.

The old man winces a little, which gives me a small sense of satisfaction, but he doesn't look away. He fixes me with his eyes, and it's a tight, unrelenting stare; and just like yesterday at the coffeehouse, I want to look away. "You look like your father," he whispers so only I can hear him.

"So," Mom almost yells, clapping her hands together, which is something she does when she's about to make an important announcement. "John was just leaving to go check out of the motel."

Thank God, I think, totally relieved. *He's leaving.*

"When you get back, John," Mom says, "I'll start dinner. Sound okay?"

"Sure thing, Grace. Thank you. That sounds wonderful."

"And while you're gone, I'll get the guest room ready for you."

The old man nods and then heads out the front door.

I feel like I'm watching a horror movie during one of those scenes when you just know something bad is about to happen to someone and you can do absolutely nothing to stop it. You just have to accept the inevitable because no matter how much you scream and point and jump up and down, the person is still going to walk right into that dark room where her miserable fate is hiding in the corner.

"Mom," I say, trailing her up the stairs. "What's going on? You didn't seriously invite him to stay here, did you? Please tell me you didn't."

"Why not?" Hayden says. He's right behind me, trying to get past me, but I keep moving from side-to-side so he can't. "You don't really want him staying at that crappy motel, do you, Parker? I've seen rats the size of small dogs running around that place. It's a dump. Seriously. It's like a hotel *took* a dump."

"Shut up, Hayden!" I yell without looking at him.

"Hay, be nice. Mrs. Rodriguez does the best she can. And Parker, don't talk to your brother like that," Mom scolds as she heads toward the guest room, which is at the very end of the hall. But when she passes the open door to my dad's office, she stops. For a moment, she just stands there, as if she's about to call for him. She doesn't, of course. Instead, she starts moving down the hall again and says to me over her shoulder, "Listen, Parker. I know it's…uncomfortable. To have him here. But we have to do this. We have to do this for Dad."

I feel a tight, sudden squeezing in my chest, like someone is pressing against me, pushing all the air out of my lungs. "You can't say what Dad would want," I wheeze. "You don't know."

Mom stops and spins around on her heels. She takes several steps toward me so that our faces are only inches apart. I'm taller than she is, but right now she feels much bigger than I am. It's strange, being this close to her. I can see the wrinkles that fan out from her eyes in a kind of cross-hatch pattern, and I can see the gray hair that's beginning to sprout near the crown of her head.

"What your father wanted, what he would have expected, is for you to treat anybody who steps into this house with respect," she practically spits at me.

I want to step away from her — I *should* step away from her — but I stay right where I am, as if my feet have been nailed to the floor. "Not for this man."

"Yes," my mom says, "*especially* for this man. Just remember, he wouldn't even be here if your father hadn't written to him."

"Exactly. Dad's the one who wanted him here. Not us."

From behind me, Hayden says, "Don't be a jerk, Parker."

I reach back and give him a shove. "Stay out of it, Hayden!"

"No!" he shouts, pushing past me and grabbing for Mom's hand. Apparently, they're a united front, and I'm just the enemy.

"Well," I say, giving up because I'm clearly not going to win this battle, "how long's he going to stay?"

"I don't know, Parker. He'll stay as long as he stays," Mom answers, her voice softening a little. "Listen, we are all in uncharted water here. Us. John. Just tell yourself that you're doing this for Dad, okay?" She touches my cheek and turns around again, heading toward the end of the hall once again.

Hayden follows her and I can hear him say, "I bet he can tell us stories about Dad, like when he was my age, don't you think?"

"Maybe," she answers. "Just don't bombard him with too many questions right away, buddy. Let him settle in a bit first, okay? Get his bearings straight."

"Yeah, okay," Hayden says before diving onto the bed and then bouncing up and down like a stupid toddler.

I just stand in the hallway, alone. Mom is right. We are in uncharted water, moving down a muddy river toward a place unknown.

CHAPTER 10

Dad's Journals

Nearly a week passes and I manage to avoid John, for the most part. The trickiest time of day is dinner because Mom pretty much demands that we eat together. There is one good thing that's come out of having an unexpected houseguest: Mom is cooking again. No more casseroles. In fact, she threw them all out. One frozen brick after another. Good intentions left to rot in our garbage can.

    Still, I hate dinner. I hate that *Grandpa John* is sitting in my father's chair. It even makes Mom fidget. It also doesn't help that the old man isn't much of a conversationalist. He mostly just sits and stares and smiles. And it's one of those closed-mouth smiles, too, so you know it's all fake. The only person he seems comfortable talking to is Hayden, but even then it's Hayden who's doing most of the talking. He fires question after question at the old man, and they're all about Dad. *What was he like? did he tell jokes? did he get into a lot of trouble? was he as good at basketball as he said he was? did he have a lot of girlfriends when he was my age? did he always like to read so much?* And on and on and on, like a goddamn blitz.

I don't even know why Hayden feels the need to ask so many questions. Dad was an open book; he'd tell you anything you wanted to know, even if it embarrassed him. Come to think of it, he especially liked to tell the embarrassing stories, the ones that ended with him flat on his face somewhere. Plus, how much could the old man possibly know, anyhow? He left.

I mumble something about this to my mom while we're cleaning up after dinner, and she just shrugs and says, "I think your brother just likes hearing about him. I do, too."

"Why doesn't Hayden just ask you then? You knew Dad when he was young, too. I mean, *God*, you started dating when you were, like, toddlers. I'm sure you could tell him plenty of stories," I say, drying a plate because the damn dishwasher decided to kick the bucket, too.

"First of all, we were not toddlers. We were thirteen," she says. "And Hayden likes listening to John because he's got different stories to tell. We all experience people in our own way."

"I guess," I say, taking another plate from her. "Do you remember him? John, I mean. From back when you first knew Dad?"

"Yes. And no. I didn't go to his house much. We all just sort of hung out at the park in town. Then when we really started dating, your dad preferred to hang out at my house."

55

"Why?"

"Because things weren't always so great there," Mom says, searching for the silverware that's hiding beneath all the soapy water.

"What do you mean?" I ask, my curiosity ready to spill over.

"Your dad's parents fought a lot. Especially as he got older."

"Why'd they fight so much? Is that why John left?"

"Look who's asking all the questions now," Mom remarks. There's no hint of playfulness in her voice, but she still splashes me with some of the dishwater, sending clusters of bubbles floating into the air. When I don't say anything back, she leans against the counter, wrapping and unwrapping a kitchen towel around her gloved hands. "I don't know why he left," she sighs. "He wasn't happy. That's all I really know."

"That's all you know, or that's all you're willing to tell me?" I stack a couple of plates in the cupboard and then slam the door so hard that it bounces back open and nearly smacks me in the face. So much for a show of indignation.

"Parker," Mom says, tossing the towel on the counter, "I really *don't* know all the details about what happened back then. Neither did your dad. But, frankly, I'm not interested in them right now. I'm just...." Her chin's shaking now and her voice suddenly sounds as if it's full of gravel, all brittle and broken up, so I know that she is trying really hard not to cry. She pulls off her dish gloves and sets them on the edge of the sink, where they hang like two limp pelts. Then she says, "It's hard enough figuring out today, let alone thirty years ago."

"I know," I say, wanting to hug her but staying put.

"Besides," Mom says, "it makes Hayden happy, having John here."

"Well, that makes one of us."

She reaches up and pats my cheek, and I can't help but notice that her hand still smells like the inside of her dish gloves, a mix of lemons and wet rubber. "Just remember that you're doing this — "

"For Dad," I interrupt. "I know."

After the conversation with my mom, I can't sleep. I toss and turn and flop around in my bed like a fish out of water. So, in the middle of the night, I sneak up to my dad's office, which is in the attic. The stairs leading up there are tight and narrow, the treads not much deeper than those of a ladder, and they scream in agony if you step on them in just the wrong spots. Fortunately, I know where all of those spots are. It does make for a more treacherous climb, having to hop and leap my way up, but it's worth it, knowing that I won't be disturbed.

The attic is huge. It runs the entire length of the house. Strangely, though, it can feel both cavernous and claustrophobic at the same time. There are windows at both the east and west ends of the room, which was Dad's favorite feature because he could watch the sunrise *and* the sunset. But his desk, just a couple of planks of red oak resting on two sawhorses, faces west because Dad preferred the softer, sinking light. "See how the sun looks like it's roosting in those maples over there?" he'd often point out, his hand resting on my shoulder.

The attic's walls are made of shiplap that's never been painted, and the floor is covered in overlapping silk and wool rugs, which are faded and worn so thin that they look more like strips of gauze in some spots. There's a sofa that slouches so much that you nearly sink to the floor when you sit in it, and there's an old, dingy recliner shoved in the corner with a floor lamp looming over it. Mostly, though, there are books. Lots and lots of books. Stacks of them. Towers of them. We used to joke with Dad that it looked like Stonehenge in here because the piles started to form a circle around the perimeter of the attic.

This is the first time I've been in my dad's office since he died. I know that Hayden's been up here a lot, though. Doing what, I don't know. But my mom won't come up here. I think she's too afraid, like she'd be jumping from a cliff without really knowing how deep the water is. Because that's what grief is like: unpredictably deep. Some days, it's so shallow that you can see the bottom, sight the dangers. Other days? Well, it's dark and cold and murky as hell.

For a long time, I just stand in the middle of the attic and breathe. It smells like my dad. Or, maybe it was my dad who smelled like the attic. I don't know. All I know is, next to coffee, this is my favorite scent in the entire world. "Dusty almonds" was how my mom once described it. Taking another deep breath, I'd have to agree.

I turn on the light near the recliner and take a quick look around, scanning my dad's bookshelves. And then I spot it: his collection of journals. "Jackpot," I whisper, pulling the wooden toolbox from its spot on the shelf. See, Dad always carried a journal with him, ever since he was thirteen. And he always used the same kind, too: a black Moleskine notebook that he could fit in his pocket. Whenever he filled one up, he added it to the box. His journals are mostly filled with daily musings and observations, favorite poems and passages, bits and pieces of conversations he might've overheard in the coffeehouse, stuff he thought he could use in a novel that he never really got around to writing. "Spend an afternoon in the coffeehouse listening to people talk, and you'll have enough material for a novel that'd put *War and Peace* to shame," he'd said not so long ago.

"Jack," Mom said in a tone she usually reserves for Hayden and me, "you're eavesdropping on people's private conversations." I'm sure she was thinking about how it might affect business, should he ever publish something in which the dialogue sounded way too familiar to the wrong customers.

Dad shrugged. "If it's so private, they shouldn't talk about it in a public space. It's nothing but fair game then."

While Dad's scribbled notes of conversations overheard in the coffeehouse are admittedly entertaining, they aren't what I'm looking for right now. I want to read about his past, see if I can find anything about the old man, maybe fill in some blanks without feeling like I'm playing the shittiest game of Mad Libs ever. Luckily for me, Dad dated all of his journals and bundled them by age, so it should be easy to find the ones I need, the ones that might offer the best clues about John. Who he was. Why he left. But when I start looking through the toolbox, I can't find them. They're gone. It's only the more recent ones that are here.

"What the hell?" I say to myself, looking two, then three more times. "Where the hell *are* they?" I almost yell, suddenly not caring if someone hears me poking around up here. I keep looking, the way you do when you discover that the thing you're looking for isn't where it's supposed to be, but you keep on rifling through the same spot, becoming increasingly convinced of one thing: Somebody must have taken it.

I slump to the floor, confused, pissed, and ready to leap to the only possible conclusion.

"That *ass*hole," I say, wondering how the old man could have been up here without any of us noticing.

CHAPTER 11

Too Much Mead

Another Friday has finally rolled around, and The Beehive is supposed to have its soft opening, which means that you can't get in without an invitation. My entire family is going, of course. Without John, I'm happy to report. He doesn't want to go. My mom tried to convince him, but only half-heartedly. Truth be told, I don't think she wanted to face having to introduce John to everyone. *Hey, this is John, Jack's father,* I can imagine her saying. *He's just here visiting with us for a while.* She'd make it sound so simple, so unencumbered. So normal.

But that's what she does. That's what she always does. She *un*complicates things. She unties stubborn knots, loosens kinks from a chain. I think that's one of the many reasons Dad loved her so much. Only, this is one time when her simple explanations just aren't good enough. There's just too much to tease out of this tangled mess of threads. I'm convinced, especially after seeing the look of relief on her face when John said that he would not be coming with us, that even she's well aware of this fact.

I haven't told her about Dad's missing journals yet. Don't get me wrong. It was the first thing I wanted to do. I practically flew down the stairs the other night, ready to drop my suspicions at her feet like a sack of rocks. But I didn't. Because, as usual, Hayden was in my parents' room, curled up in his spot in the corner. Then, as if everything in the universe was hell-bent on conspiring against me, I remembered what my mom had said: *It makes Hayden happy having him here.*

So I've kept my discovery to myself. For now.

Anyway, the opening of the meadery is a success. The Beehive is actually pretty close to the coffeehouse, but it's tucked away near the back of the building with its main entrance in the alley, which they've festooned with white and yellow paper lanterns for the party. The inside of the meadery is pretty small, but it's perfect. The perfect representation of my dad, that is. It's both modern and rustic, new and old. My dad, like my mom, loved history and anything with a good story to tell; but he also loved weird, contemporary stuff, too. He had no problem, for instance, pairing clear plastic chairs with old, antique tables, which is exactly what he and Leo did in the meadery. The pendant lights, which they designed themselves, are made from those aqua-blue glass insulators that used to sit like birds on the cross-arms of old telephone poles. We actually spent last summer scouring flea market after flea market for them. Leo decided to hang them at different lengths, which sort of makes it feel like there are glowing, iridescent bubbles floating through the air.

But it's the bar itself that's really impressive. My dad spent months building it in our garage. He used his old wood-burning tools, stuff that he'd had since he was a kid, on slabs of oak to make it look like honeycomb. Then he stained them, framed them, and covered them with a thick layer of epoxy. The bar looks like a giant piece of preserved honeycomb, like amber that's been mined. It's beautiful. Seeing it, I can't help but slide my hand across its glassy surface. I close my eyes, just for a second, and remember my dad hunched over it, quiet with concentration, proud of a job well done.

"Hey, kid," I hear a familiar voice say. It's Leo. He's basically the older version of Charlie. Bearded. Tattooed. Cool.

"Hey," I say back, trying to muster up a smile.

Leo hands me a small glass of mead. "Here," he says, "try it."

"Are you sure?" I say, a little surprised and quickly checking to see where my mom might be.

Leo nods and then holds up his own taller glass of mead, saying, "Cheers. To your dad. We wouldn't even have this place if it wasn't for him."

We clink glasses and drink. The mead is good. It's sweet and kind of tastes like spring.

I sit down at the bar and decide to just people watch. Sometimes I don't mind just "holding up the wall," as my mom would say. She and Hayden are across the room, talking with Haywood's mayor, Greg Hutchins. He's a regular at the coffeehouse and always orders the same thing: vanilla latte, extra shot of espresso. And he never tips. Unless he's up for re-election, that is. Then he manages to relinquish a buck or so, but not without cringing at the sound of the coins hitting the bottom of the jar, the one we very cleverly labeled with a sign that reads, SUPPORT COUNTER INTELLIGENCE.

Anyway, I'm watching my mom and brother talk to this tool when Charlie takes a seat next to me. He's dressed in jeans, a T-shirt, and a gray suit jacket. I am suddenly and painfully aware that I am underdressed in my wrinkled shorts (which I dug out of the hamper) and sweatshirt. "Well," he says, slapping me on the back. "Whaddya think?" he grins.

"Are you buzzed?" I ask, not realizing my pun until it's too late.

"As a matter of fact, I am. Care to join me?"

I shrug. "Why not."

Charlie hops off the stool and walks behind the bar. He takes my glass and fills it. "Bee Spit," he says as he slides it back to me. "Enjoy."

"Thanks." I take a sip. I can tell right away that it's not the same brew that Leo had given me. It has a sharper edge to it. More bitter somehow.

"Good?" Charlie asks, filling his own glass again.

"Yeah. Thanks." I take another sip. "The name's still terrible, though."

After downing a few more samples, I start to feel pretty good. Nice and lightheaded. But it doesn't last long because before I know it, my mom is right next to me. And needless to say, she is not happy.

"*Parker*!" she whispers through clenched teeth. "Do you want the place to be shut down before they even open?!"

"No," I answer, grinning stupidly. I don't mean to. I really don't think it's funny. It's just the mead.

"Then what do you think you're doing?"

"Sorry, Aunt Grace," Charlie says, saving me. "It's my fault. I figured it'd be okay for him to try a few samples. I didn't realize I'd given him so much."

My mom relaxes a little. I can tell that she isn't completely convinced, but she's willing to accept Charlie's explanation because it's the easier thing to do right now. Plus, she hates any kind of arguing in public. She says it's trashy.

"Why don't I take him over to the coffee shop? We could both use a little espresso. Right, Parker?" Charlie offers.

"Yeah," I say, doing my best to steady myself against the counter.

Mom nods in agreement. "Good idea. Madge is training the new girl I hired."

This gets my attention. "You hired somebody? I didn't know you were going to do that." My tone is a bit more forceful than I had intended; it sounds a little too much like an accusation.

"I didn't know that I needed your permission, Parker," my mom says as she starts rifling through her bag for something. She does, however, flash me a quick look, the kind that's meant to put me in my place.

I've had enough mead to think about reminding her that

I'm the official Man of the House now, but not enough to make me actually say it. It's bullshit, anyway. It's just something that well-meaning adults say to make you feel better, like it should be a consolation that your opinion might suddenly matter more now. Well, guess what? It doesn't. My opinion weighs the same as it did before my dad died. I guess that for my mom, there's only ever been one Man of the House, and that's fine by me. I don't want the title, anyway.

Charlie and I say goodbye to everyone and head over to The Mill. Madge is at the register with the new girl showing her how to ring up orders. When she sees us, she smiles and waves. Behind me I hear Charlie say, in a whisper laced with both desperation and lust, "I seriously need to ask your mother to change my work schedule."

Knowing exactly what he means, I say, "Not like you'd have a chance." But truth be told, he probably *would* have a chance with Madge, which makes me just a little bit jealous.

"Hey, guys," Madge says. "How was The Beehive?"

"Great," Charlie says. "Too bad you had to work."

Madge smiles. "I know. But somebody's gotta hold down the fort."

"Can you make us two espressos, Madge?" I ask, grinning stupidly again.

Madge reaches across the counter, grabs my chin, and sort of moves my head side-to-side, studying my face. "Are you drunk?" she asks.

"Nah," Charlie chimes in. "This little bee is just a-buzzin'."

"Oh, my God," she says, releasing my chin with a jerk. "I

thought your mom was going to the opening."

"She went," I say.

Madge shakes her head with disapproval. "You are shameless."

"Who's this?" Charlie asks, changing the subject.

"Oh," Madge smiles. "This is Murphy."

"Murphy, eh?" Charlie nods. "Cool name."

"Thanks," Murphy says. She's young, probably my age, but I don't recognize her. She's short with long, blond, poker-straight hair. There's one spot above her left ear that's been shaved, which you'd think would give her an edgy look, except that she's got these big brown eyes that are framed by a bright pink pair of glasses. This juxtaposition is kind of jarring, but it somehow works. Suddenly, I find myself thinking that the new girl is kind of pretty.

"Hi," I finally say. "I'm Parker."

"The owner's son," Madge says over her shoulder as she pulls two espresso cups from the shelf.

"Oh," Murphy says, without any kind of alarm. "I think I'm scheduled to work with you tomorrow."

"Cool," I nod. The way she's looking at me, I think she expects me to say something else, but I've got nothing. I sort of point to the couch to indicate that that's where I'm heading, which works, because she turns her back to me and starts talking to Madge again.

Charlie and I sink into the couch and put our feet up on the coffee table. When Madge brings us our espressos, we sip them in silence. Then Charlie says, "So how are things on the home front?"

"You mean what's it like living with a total stranger?" I respond. I'm leaning against the back of the couch now with my eyes closed. Thankfully, the room isn't spinning.

"He's not a stranger."

I sit up. "Yes he is. Actually, he's worse. He's, like, an *interloper*."

"Nice word. Very SAT of you."

"Thanks. I try."

"Seriously, though. It's not like he's trying to *replace* your dad. Because that would be fucked up, no doubt. The guy just has really shitty timing."

"The worst."

For a while, we just sit. I consider telling him about the missing journals but choose the silence instead. Honestly, Charlie is one of the few people I can spend a considerable amount of time with in absolute silence and not start to feel completely weird or uncomfortable. Even with Noah and Dante, the silence demands to be disrupted at some point. It has to be. With them, words are like buoys, holding us up when the silence sends us sinking. But not with Charlie. With him, I've always been able to just float.

CHAPTER 12

Sitting in the Dark

When I get home, everything is dark and quiet, except for one familiar noise: the dishwasher. It's fixed. "Who fixed the dishwasher?" I holler, fully expecting Mom to answer.

"I did," John says. He's sitting in the dark at the kitchen table eating toast. (Seriously, who eats toast at ten o'clock at night? Let alone *plain* toast?)

"Oh," I say. Then, begrudgingly, "Thanks."

"You're welcome. I told your mom it's the least I can do."

"Yeah, well. Great." I'm not sure what else to say. I look around the room because I don't want to look directly at him. The darkness, you see, makes it dangerous to look at him. It softens his wrinkles and hides his balding head. It makes him look too much like Dad.

I hit the switch on the wall, and he's the old man again.

He squints a little, the light offending his tired eyes. "You mind dimming that a little?" he asks.

"Sure." I turn the knob and the lights obey, shrinking to a soft glow.

"Thanks," John says. He starts to rub his fingers. I've noticed that he does this a lot, but I haven't figured out if it's because his knuckles, which are fat and swollen, are sore; or if it's simply because he's nervous. Or guilty. Or all of the above.

"Well," I say, "I'm going to bed."

"Wait. Parker. I was hoping…I was hoping that maybe we could spend a little time together. I thought maybe we could…go fishing or something."

"Fishing?"

"Yes."

I imagine the two of us cramped in a little canoe in the middle of a lake, bobbing up and down. John's at the bow, and I'm at the stern. Then I see — because imagination and memory are sometimes sneaky partners — my father paddling past us in his kayak. He's waving at me, at us. Then he's clutching at his chest, flipping over in his kayak, being swallowed up by the dark, murky water.

"I don't fish," I say, which is a lie.

Just then, Hayden runs down the hall and into the kitchen. "Hey, John! You wanna play a video game with me?"

John looks at his hands. "I'm not sure I can. My hands are awfully sore after working on the dishwasher."

"No problem," Hayden says. "C'mon. We can play *Most Wanted*."

"Sounds...criminal."

"It's just a racing game. But you *do* have to race away from the police. I'll let you use the wheel. You *can* drive, can't you?"

"How do you think I got here?"

"Good point," Hayden says, leading the way.

They disappear down the hall, as if swept away by some invisible current.

CHAPTER 13

Harry Versus Luke

After working a couple of shifts with Murphy at the coffeehouse, I have discovered a few things about her. First, her full name is Abigail Murphy McMillan. She was named after her mother, who shares the exact same name, except that she goes by Abigail. To avoid any confusion, her mother decided to just call Murphy by her middle name. The name fits her perfectly, though. She doesn't wear any makeup, and I've yet to see her wear any kind of jewelry, unless you count earbuds as an accessory. She also pretty much wears a self-imposed uniform of dark jeans, Vans sneakers, and an impressive rotation of concert T-shirts. Oh, and those bright pink glasses.

The second thing I've discovered about Murphy is that she is a quick learner. And she's fast on her feet, too. She sort of reminds me of a woodland sprite, quick and light on the toes, able to fly about a room without much trouble. Of course, the fact that she's quite small — not *little* person small, but definitely not taller than five feet — adds to this effect. "She looks like she'd fit into your pocket," Madge says, and I'd have to agree.

Even though Murphy and I go to different schools — she goes to Glendale, our rival, if you're into that kind of thing — our final exam schedules are essentially the same, which means that we've both been able to pick up extra hours in the last, lingering weeks of school. So, on a rainy afternoon, when it's not too busy, I decide to show her how to use Clyde, our espresso machine.

"Are you sure?" she asks. "I mean, are you sure your mom won't mind?"

"Nah," I say, waving my hand, brushing away her concern. "She trusts my judgment. Plus, she's even said that she thinks you're doing a great job."

"Really?"

"Yeah." This compliment seems to make her happy because a smile tugs at both corners of her mouth.

I show her how to fill the portafilter basket with the grounds and then how to level them off with her finger. I tell her to tamp the grounds once with the heel of her hand while I flush some of the water through the machine to let it cool just a bit. Murphy then locks the filter into place and turns the espresso machine on. Clyde is a semi-automatic machine, so making the perfect espresso is really just a matter of timing. After just a few attempts, Murphy manages to make a very respectable shot of espresso. Like I said, she's a quick learner.

"When do I get to learn how to do foam?" she asks, eager to learn more, to advance to the next step.

"Patience, padawan," I say, tapping her lightly on the head. It's irresistible since she's so much shorter than I am.

Her eyebrows cinch together. "Padawan?" she asks.

I just look at her, incredulous. "Yeah. You know. Like a Jedi knight in training."

"Ohhhh. It's a *Star Wars* reference," she says. "Sorry. Never been my thing. I just don't get what the big deal is."

I lay my hand across my chest and pretend to stumble backward into the counter. "That's like a dagger to the heart! Seriously. You essentially just crapped on my entire childhood."

"What can I say? I'm more of a *Harry Potter* fan."

"*C'mon*! Really? No way is that scar-faced nerd cooler than Luke Skywalker. Or Han Solo, for that matter."

"Uh, yeah. He most definitely is. Plus, I'd take a wand over a lightsaber any day."

I smile and grab one of the foot-long barista spoons and start waving it around like I'm Luke Skywalker, doing my best to mimic the wavy, electric sound of a lightsaber. "*Wshhhhh!*" I say as I swing the spoon over my head with both hands firmly clasped around the end of it.

Murphy takes her own spoon from the counter, points it at me, and says, with a devilish grin on her face, "Avada Kedavra."

"What's that mean? That your secret wizard name or something?" I say, still poised to battle her.

"Nope. Basically, I just killed you."

"Huh?"

Murphy, still wearing her evil smirk, says, "Avada Kedavra. From *Harry Potter*. It's a spell to kill a person."

"Wow," I say. "Guess you're just a cold, heartless little wizard."

"Hey. I told you. Wand trumps lightsaber. Every. Damn. Time."

The door to the shop opens. It's Noah and Dante. I realize that I'm still holding the spoon, so I set it down on the counter again. "Hey," I call to them.

"Afternoon," Noah says, tossing his hair back with a quick jerk. Now that his bangs are a little longer, he's developed the very annoying habit of jerking his head to the side to coax the curtain of hair out of his eyes.

"Hey," Dante says.

"Do you two want to order anything? Espresso maybe?" Murphy asks, a gleam in her eye.

Oh, boy, I think. *I've created a monster.*

"No, thanks," Dante answers. "Just two regular coffees. To go."

"What's going on later?" I ask. "Anything interesting?"

Noah accepts his coffee from Murphy. "Only the usual."

"No plans with Lisa then?" I ask.

"Nah. I'm taking a little hiatus from Her Majesty," Noah says with a sour tone.

Dante, who's pouring obscene amounts of cream and sugar into his coffee, says, "We're hanging out at Gabe and Tony's. You coming?"

"Probably later. My mom's been making us all eat

dinner together," I answer, rolling my eyes.

Dante and Noah nod, but it's Noah who says, "So, how's that going? With your grandfather, I mean?"

"For the record, I don't call him that," I say.

"Okay," Dante says, "what do you call him then?"

Before I can answer, Murphy chimes in with "He-Who-Must-Not-Be-Named?"

We all look at her, confused. "Never mind," she says, waving her hand in disgust.

"I don't call him anything," I say. This is absolutely true. Since John has been here, I have never once addressed him by his name, and I certainly refuse to call him Grandfather. It is a title that he does not deserve. I mean, think about it: He was neither a father to my dad, nor is he in any way *grand*.

Noah and Dante both nod again. They get it. Especially Noah. His father was dead for less than a year when his mother remarried. She'd gone to Pennsylvania for a long weekend, "To see an old high school friend," she'd said, and came back married. For months, Noah simply referred to the guy as The Asshole. He'd say things like, "My mom and The Asshole are going out of town," or "My mom and The Asshole are buying a new car." That was a long time ago, though. Nearly three years. Now he calls his stepfather by his first name: Randy. "Randy is just dandy," Noah often says. It's kind of a required mantra. His mother eventually got tired of him referring to her new husband as The Asshole, so she basically told him that if he didn't stop, she was going to have to choose between the two of them. "So choose," Noah had said to her, confident he knew what she'd do. But all she'd said was "Noah, you really don't want me to do that."

So, yes, Noah gets it. He knows what it's like to have someone invade his space.

"So we'll definitely see you later tonight then?" he asks as he and Dante head toward the door.

"Sure," I call back.

When they're outside, Murphy says, "I like your friends. They seem pretty chill."

"They are." Then I say, "You want to hang out with us later?"

Murphy smiles. "Sure."

"No killing spells, though," I tease, pointing a spoon at her again.

Still smiling, she says, "I make no promises."

CHAPTER 14

Fighting with Mom

When I walk into the kitchen, John is standing at the stove. He has a kitchen towel thrown over his left shoulder and an apron tied loosely around his waist. He's cooking. In our kitchen. And, I have to admit, there's nothing about this scenario that feels right. I mean, once you start cooking in someone's kitchen, opening their drawers, rifling through their cupboards, you've reached an entirely new level of comfort and familiarity. You are no longer a guest. You are *one of the family*.

And I'm sure as hell not ready for the old man to be counted as one of the family.

"Parker," he says when he sees me, "I hope you're hungry. I've made enough soup to feed an army."

"You made soup? It's, like, almost eighty degrees out."

"True. But it's raining. And rain always makes me want

soup." He turns around and gives the soup a quick stir before setting the wooden spoon on the counter and then sitting down on the chair that he's dragged to the stove. Apparently, stirring soup is strenuous work.

I shake my head to myself and think, *Toast at night? Soup when it's hot outside?* One thing is for certain: The old man has some strange eating habits.

I start to head upstairs when I hear my mom call for me from her office, which is across from the living room. She's at her roll-top desk looking through what I can only assume is a stack of bills. When she sees me, she offers a quick smile and says, "How was the coffeehouse? Busy or no?"

"Eh. Okay. I showed Murphy how to make espresso."

"How'd she do?"

"Not bad, actually."

She takes off her reading glasses, just one of many cheap pairs that she's purchased from the pharmacy, and tosses them on her desk. "John's making dinner."

"Yeah. I know. Soup." I roll my eyes.

"Be nice," she warns, pointing a finger at me. Mom gets up from her chair and moves to a different pile of papers. She's looking for something. But it's not bills she's looking through this time. It's cards and letters, condolences people sent us when Dad died.

"What're you looking for?" I ask, taking a few steps toward her.

But she ignores my question and says, "Parker. I want you to at least try with John. I want you to be nicer. I want you to be...*you*." She waves her hand at me, as if she can erase the son who's standing in front of her and conjure up the one she remembers.

"I *am* being me," I say. I can hear the whiny edge in my voice, the defensive tone.

"No you're not, Parker," my mom snaps back. "You're acting like someone I don't even know."

A prickly feeling crawls up my spine and a wave of heat rushes through my chest, spreading to my throat and then my face. "There is someone you don't know in this house, but it's not me, Mom. It's *him*," I say through gritted teeth, pointing toward the kitchen and fighting the urge to yell. "The guy could be a criminal for all we know. He's probably...he's probably in there poisoning our *soup*. Think about it, Mom. How *convenient* that he shows up after — "

"You're not even giving him a chance. He's not as bad as you think he is, you know."

"He stole Dad's journals!" I blurt out.

Mom looks at me, her forehead cinched tight in the middle. "What are you talking about?"

"Dad's journals. From when he was young? I went up to the attic the other night, and they weren't there. John took them. He had to've." *Boom!* I think, suddenly tempted to pace the room like a badass lawyer who's got this case in the bag.

"Why would you want to go through Dad's journals?" she asks, clearly missing my point.

"Mom," I say, frustrated and more than a little deflated, "that's not the point. The point is that John — "

"No, Parker. The point is that you went snooping through your dad's stuff."

"I wouldn't call it snooping. I'd call it investigating."

"Investigating what?"

From the kitchen, John calls, "Soup's on!"

"*Him*!" I whisper-yell.

Mom shakes her head, slowly. "Oh, Jesus, Parker."

"What?" I growl. "I want to figure this guy out."

Mom throws her hands in the air and sort of shakes them at me. "Then *talk* to him," she says, like it's that simple.

"Oh, so he can just tell me a bunch of lies? Mom, Dad's journals might tell us something about him. That's why he went up there and stole them. He's hiding something. I know it."

"John hasn't even been up to the attic. You're just…you're just being ridiculous. And paranoid, I might add."

"*I'm* being ridiculous?! I'm not the one who let a stranger move in with us!"

"He's not a *stranger*."

"Yes, he freaking is!" I now understand why so many fights in the movies end with someone throwing something because that's seriously all I want to do right now. I want the satisfaction of watching something break into a thousand little pieces.

Mom points at me and says, "Your brother likes John. He's getting to know him. *He's* giving him a chance. Perhaps you should think about doing the same. Maybe then you'll get all the answers you need."

"Mom, *c'mon*," I beg. "What kind of person just up and leaves his family without so much as a note? I'm sorry, but I will never understand it, and I will never forgive it."

Mom leans against her desk and crosses her arms. "Parker, maybe what you need to remember here is that whatever John did isn't for you to forgive."

"Exactly," I say with deliberate volume. "But the one who can forgive him isn't here, is he? He's *dead*!"

I feel the smack before I hear it. Immediately, my cheek starts to burn and my eyes water.

"Oh, my God," Mom whispers, reaching for me. "I'm so sorry. Parker, I'm — "

"No," I say, moving away from her, out of her reach.

"Parker, *please*."

"Just...just stay away from me." And then I leave. I just walk out because, right now, it's the only thing I can think to do.

CHAPTER 15

The Shed

For a long time, I just walk around town. Thankfully, the rain has finally stopped. Blades of light cut through the clouds, and little puffs of steam rise from the warm pavement like ghosts. For a moment, I allow myself to imagine my dad walking next to me, and I hear him tell me how the wet pavement reminds him of mercury glass. "See how it's dull in some spots? Shimmering in others?" he'd say.

Because that's what he did. He always found a way to connect one thing to another.

I rub at my cheek, which still stings a little. I should be pissed at my mom, but I'm not. I actually feel sorry for her. She's never hit me, and I've never walked out after arguing with her. So I guess it's official: We've both reached a new low.

I decide that there's just one person to blame for our bad

behavior, and it's none other than the old man.

At seven o'clock, I stop by the coffeehouse to pick up Murphy, who's already waiting by the door when I get there. "Ah, padawan," I say, trying my best to sound cheerful and absolutely unaffected by what happened with my mom (and hoping that there isn't a handprint on my left cheek).

"Seriously?" Murphy says, adjusting her glasses. "We're still on that?"

"Yes," I say, "the Force is strong in you."

"Huh?"

"Eh. Never mind."

Charlie and Madge are behind the counter. It's their turn to close tonight. When Charlie sees me, he says, "Well, well, well. What do we have here?"

"Nothing," I say, a bit too quickly.

"We're just going to hang out," Murphy adds.

"What exactly, may I ask, is going to 'hang out'?" Charlie asks, a dumb grin on his face. Charlie doesn't have very many vices, but one of them is his penchant for really bad sexual innuendo. Usually at my expense. I guess this is what I get for always wishing that he'd been my big brother.

Madge, who is not a big fan of stupid humor, punches Charlie in the shoulder, hard.

"What?" he says, rubbing his shoulder. "He knows I'm just messin' with him!"

"But Murphy doesn't," Madge points out, coming to Murphy's rescue.

"Sorry, Murph," Charlie says with sincerity. "I apologize. I suppose that wasn't very gentleman-like of me. Please do forgive me." He bows for an added bit of drama.

Murphy laughs a little. "That's okay." Then she looks at me with a slight simper. "I'll bet he doesn't have much to 'hang out' anyway," she says, nudging me with her elbow.

"*Ohhhh!*" Charlie covers his mouth with his fist and then laughs with approval. Madge, however, just rolls her eyes and turns on Bonnie, the grinder. It's what she does when she's annoyed; it's basically her way of telling us all to shut the hell up.

We leave the coffeehouse and head toward Gabe and Tony's house. It occurs to me then that Murphy hasn't met the twins yet. "I think you'll like them," I tell her. "They don't say very much, so there isn't really much to *dislike*."

"Actually, I did meet them. At The Mill. They were studying or something. They were speaking Spanish mostly, so I didn't really catch most of what they were talking about."

"Oh. Well. That's good then. I mean, not that you didn't understand them, but that you met them."

Everybody's already there when we arrive. Gabe and Tony; Noah and Dante; even Victor and Sarah. With this many people, the shed is a little more cramped than usual. It wasn't always this way. When we were younger, it used to feel enormous. It felt like the entire world could fit into it. Well, our entire world, anyway.

Now, it can barely hold us.

"Who's this?" Victor asks, lifting his chin in Murphy's direction. I try to ignore the fact that Sarah is sitting on his lap.

"This is Murphy. She works at the coffeehouse with

me," I say.

"Murphy?" Sarah says, smiling (and rubbing Victor's thigh). "That's a different name. Cool, though. I like it."

"Thanks," Murphy says before squeezing herself into a spot on the floor.

Victor has managed to score us some beer. Not the cheap, watered-down stuff, either. "My dad bought it," he announces, pulling some bottles from a cooler that doubles as a chair, a chair that Victor tends to treat as his throne. When he's around, no one else is really allowed to sit there, especially when it's holding beer. He likes to be the one in charge of distributing any and all drinks, which really only ensures that he takes more for himself.

"Your dad bought you beer?" asks Dante, unable to hide his doubt.

"Yep. Let's just say he didn't really have much of a choice."

"What's that supposed to mean?" Tony asks, opening his bottle. "You blackmail him or something?"

Victor snaps a bottle cap between his fingers, and it ricochets around the shed. "Pretty much."

"Yeah," Sarah chimes in, "he threatened to tell his dad's new girlfriend that he saw him at Mary's trying to pick up some girl who's, like, *our age*." Mary's is the local greasy spoon, and it's right across the street from The Mill. It's good for a mediocre burger and soggy fries and that's about it.

"Is that even true?" Noah says, already beginning to peel the label from his bottle of beer. He likes to see if he can remove the entire label cleanly so that he can add it to his collection in the corner of the shed where he's started his own makeshift wallpapering project.

Victor takes a long swig of his beer. "Absolutely."

Like father, like son, I think, wanting to warn Sarah that that could be her future if she insists on giving Victor too many chances.

Victor holds up his bottle. "Cheers, men. Oh, and ladies, of course." We all hold up our bottles, too, and drink. The beer is strong, but it tastes pretty good.

The rest of the night glides along, sort of slow and smooth. We do the usual: talk, listen to music, play cards. Victor is pretty lit, having drunk most of the beer that he brought; and when Victor's had too many, he turns mean. Meaner than usual, I should say. Tonight, because she's new here, he sets his sights on Murphy.

"So," he belches, "Murphy. What kind of name is that, anyway?"

"It was my mom's maiden name," she answers very matter-of-factly.

Victor snorts. "Sorry, but it kinda sounds like a dog's name."

Gabe glances at Victor and says, "No seas un pendejo con ella."

"In English," Victor demands.

"It means don't be an asshole," Tony says as he shuffles a deck of cards.

"Yeah," Sarah warns. "Don't."

"Well," Murphy says, "I'm *sorry*, but Victor kinda sounds like a winner's name."

"Your point?" Victor asks, downing the last of his beer.

She stands up and brushes off the back of her pants. "That *you* seem like a loser."

Sarah looks at me. Her lips are pressed together because she's trying not to laugh. And I want nothing more than to hand Murphy a gold medal.

CHAPTER 16

Dad's Letter

It's past midnight when I get home. The backdoor is unlocked, so I know that my mom must still be awake, waiting for me, which sucks because I really don't want to see her. I'm in no mood (or state of mind, frankly) to deal with a lecture or hand out the apology that I know I owe her.

When I go upstairs, the light is on in my room. *Shit. She's in there*, I think, and the beer that's sloshing around in my stomach turns sour and threatens to climb up my throat. I hesitate when I reach my door, but eventually push it open a bit wider, expecting to see her sitting on my bed, but she's not there.

Instead, on my bed is a letter. Two letters, actually. The first one is from my mom; but the other one — the one that really catches my eye and stops my breath — is from my dad.

First, I read the letter — well, *note* is probably a better word — from Mom. It says, *I'm sorry. If you read this letter that your dad wrote, you'll understand. I hope.*

So, I do what she says. I start to read the letter, expecting to see my name scribbled across the top. But it isn't there. It's addressed to Dad. *His* dad.

Dear Dad,
I don't even know where to start, so I guess I'll just start by saying that I've been looking for you for a while now. After all these years, you probably never expected to hear from me, but I have thought of you countless times. Nearly every day, in fact. I would be lying if I said that I wasn't angry with you for leaving us. But life has been good to me, and I have learned over time to forgive you.

Do you remember Grace? Well, I married her. You were right back then. She was a catch! Still is, actually. We have two sons, Parker and Hayden. Parker just turned seventeen. He reminds me so much of myself when I was that age. He's smart and stubborn and loyal. And Hayden? He's an eleven-year-old with a wicked sense of humor and a killer imagination.

I guess that's why I really wanted to find you. If you're willing, I'd like to see you, to have you meet our boys, your grandsons. It's not too late. We can make things right.

I've included our numbers and our address.

Please, if you want to, call me. I'd love to talk with you, to hear your voice.

Love,
Jackie

It seems weird, but the first thing I focus on is how my dad signed the letter. *Jackie?* I wonder. The first time John referred to my father, that's what he'd called him. Now, here's a letter signed by my father using the same nickname, a nickname that I have never heard anyone else call him, not even Mom. It feels kind of like a betrayal. Or like I've been left out of something, at least. I've always thought of nicknames as things that are given and shared between friends and family. They're like unofficial titles of love and friendship, like you aren't part of the squad until someone has decided to change your name, even if it's only dropping a syllable. Or adding one, apparently.

"Jackie," I say to myself, trying it out. *Kinda sounds like a girl's name*, I can hear Victor saying.

I look at the letter again. Actually, I stare at it, nearly mesmerized. I knew it existed, of course. I knew that my father had supposedly written to the old man, but I hadn't accepted it as fact. Not really.

"Hey, Parker." My mom is standing in the doorway. She looks tired, and like she's been crying.

"Mom," I say, setting the letter down. "I'm sorry."

"Me, too, buddy." She steps into my room and sits next to me on the bed, Dad's letter resting between us. She reaches over and tucks a piece of hair behind my ear; then she sort of pets my head, the way she used to do when I was younger and had trouble falling asleep. "John gave me the letter the first day he was here," she says. "I should have shown it to you then. I guess I just thought that it would upset you even more. I'm sorry."

"I'm not sure it would have made much of a difference then."

"Does it now?" she asks, looking at me.

"I don't know. Maybe."

Mom turns so that she's facing me and grabs both of my hands. "Parker. Let it make a difference. Please." I don't recognize this look on her face; it's one that I've never seen before. Then I realize what she's doing: She is pleading with me.

I relent. How can I not? "Okay," I whisper. "For Dad."

She kisses my cheek, the one she smacked earlier, and says, "Thank you."

"But...."

"But what?"

I'm almost too afraid to ask, but I do anyway because I'm still being fueled by some liquid courage. "What about Dad's journals?"

Mom smiles. "Hayden's got them."

"What?"

"Hayden's got them. After you left, I went up to his room, and there they were."

"Oh."

"He's starting his own journal. About Dad."

"Oh," I say again, feeling like a major jackass.

"It's okay, Parker. You believed John took them because you wanted to be right about him. You wanted to prove that he's — "

"No good? evil? not to be trusted?" I offer, smiling a bit, so she knows I'm only joking now. Kind of.

She squeezes my knee and then stands up to leave. "We're doing the right thing. Your dad would be proud. Of all of us."

"Did you look at them? The journals, I mean?"

"Yes, Parker. I've read them. Your dad always let me read his journals," Mom says, like I've insulted her or something.

"Nothing incriminating then, huh?"

Mom smiles a little now. "Nope," she says before kissing me on the forehead.

"All right," I sigh.

Before she walks out the door, she turns and says, "Look at the envelope, too, Parker."

"Yeah. Okay," I say. I'm not totally convinced that giving the old man a chance is the right thing to do; and based on the lack of conviction in my mom's voice, I doubt that she's totally convinced, either. But I know she's doing her best to lead us through this fog, hoping — like I am — that Dad's spirit is somehow guiding her, like a beam of light slicing through the mist.

I lie down and read the letter over and over again. I let my fingers follow the shape of my dad's words. I study them, as if they're some ancient text recorded on a stiff piece of parchment. The letters are neater than usual, and the words more carefully spaced out. There is nothing scratched out, nor is there a letter that's been corrected with an extra loop or line. My dad must have written this letter many, many times. He must have studied his own words and wondered at them. He must have hesitated for a moment as he dropped the letter in the mail, listened to it sink into a sea of letters, hoping that it would find its way to shore.

I set the letter on my chest and watch it rise and fall with each breath, its edges fluttering like a leaf in the wind. I sit up then to look for the envelope, which I find lying on the floor next to my bed.

It's postmarked *21 March 2019.*

The day my dad died.

CHAPTER 17

The Scoop

"No way," Charlie says when I tell him.

"Yes. The day he died."

"Wow."

"I know."

Madge says, "It's a sign. You know that, right?"

"Maybe," I admit with obvious reluctance.

"Oh, *c'mon!*" Madge yells. As usual, she's got receipts and scraps of paper stuffed into the pockets of her jeans. I wonder when she might string together some of her daily musings. She must have enough to write an epic at this point. Then again, that may not be the best idea for the rest of us. She's wearing a shirt today that says, CAREFUL OR YOU'LL END UP IN MY NOVEL. Not such a veiled threat, I guess.

Charlie slaps me on the shoulder. "Seriously, man. Take

it as a sign. From your — "

"Don't say it," I beg, holding up my hand to stop him. "I already know."

My first attempt at bonding with John is awkward, but it's tempered by the fact that Hayden is with us. Mom suggested that we go out for ice cream, so that's what we're doing, walking to Main Street for ice cream. For most of the walk, I trail behind Hayden and the old man, hoping that we don't see anyone. I haven't actually introduced John to any of my friends. He's kind of made it easy to avoid since he hasn't come back to the coffeehouse since that first day. To be honest, he hasn't really gone much farther than the front porch.

Hayden talks the entire time, of course. He points out people's houses, tells the old man who lives in them, what they do, if they have any strange habits, even any secrets they may be hiding. You see, Hayden started his own lawn service last summer, which consisted mostly of weeding people's gardens, so he often found himself crouched beneath their open windows, privy to conversations that he definitely was not supposed to hear. Last summer, he'd come home and entertain us with his stories until Mom finally told him that he was becoming nothing more than the town gossip. Dad, however, salivated over the stories. Really, what I think he loved most was hearing Hayden tell them. He's a great storyteller, just like Dad was. One of our dad's favorite stories from last summer was the one about the O'Connors and how Mrs. O'Connor would cut her husband's hair in their backyard only to force him to rake up the bright red clippings from the grass while she looked on from their deck, a tall glass of lemonade sweating in her hand. It was a good story, and one that made Dad utter one of his favorite lines: "The truth is stranger than fiction."

Anyway, that's what Hayden's doing now with John: telling him stories.

Since it's a warm, humid evening, The Scoop is crowded, the line trailing down the sidewalk and curving around the corner. *Great*, I think. *More time to bond.*

Sarah is here, too, with some little girl I don't know. "Hi!" she waves as we pass her.

"Hey." I move quickly, wanting to avoid introductions, but Hayden thwarts my plan.

"Hi, Hayden," Sarah says, giving him a quick high five.

Hayden steps away from Sarah and does exactly what I didn't want him to do: He introduces Sarah to John. "Sarah," he smiles, "this is our grandpa, John." (Yes, Hayden is already referring to him as our grandpa.)

"Hi," says Sarah, throwing me a quick look. "Nice to meet you."

"You, too," John says, shaking her hand.

Thankfully, the little girl that Sarah is babysitting tugs violently at her arm, so they move along, leaving us to find a spot at the back of the line.

"Hoppin' place," John says.

Hayden can't stand still. Ice cream, even the mere thought of it, makes the kid hyper. "I'm gonna get a vanilla-chocolate swirl in a cup with gummy bears," he announces.

"Gross, bro," I say.

"What about you, Parker?" John asks. He's got his hands in his pockets; and, despite the warm temperature, he's wearing an old, tattered sweater and a dark green golf cap that's seen better days. If he doesn't feel like our grandfather, he certainly looks the part.

"Uh, chocolate shake, I guess." Then, because I told my mother that I would try, I say, "And you?"

"Me? Just a vanilla cone. I'm a simple man when it comes to ice cream."

Hayden stops moving. "That's what Dad always used to get, too," he says, as if he's heard the most amazing thing ever.

John smiles. "Really? Well, that's what he always ordered when he was your age. Didn't change much, did he?"

How the hell would you know? I think.

Twenty minutes later, we're walking back home with our ice cream. Hayden nearly drops his several times because he's jumping over cracks on the sidewalk and practicing various soccer moves. (I think Dante is his Charlie, which doesn't really bother me. Too much.) What this really means is that I'm stuck walking with John.

"I like this town. Reminds me a little of where I used to live," John says before biting into his cone.

"Oh yeah? With Dad?" I ask. "Or somewhere else?" Of course, I've been to Mom and Dad's hometown, Orchard Ridge, many times. It's not that far away, just over an hour. My mom's parents still live there; and so did my dad's mom, when she was still alive. I never knew her because she died just a few months after I was born. She'd been sick and was just waiting for a chance to hold her grandson. That's what my parents always told me, anyway.

Orchard Ridge is very similar to Haywood. Their Main Streets are nearly identical, each of them lined with pizza shops and dress shops and antique stores and dingy little auto parts stores. Of course, there's also the obligatory liquor store on the corner and the occasional empty store with a FOR RENT sign propped in a dirty window. There are also the same banners stretched across each Main Street like sails, boasting about the local marching band or announcing an upcoming event that's meant for old people or families with toddlers. And, since the towns were built around the same time, the architecture is pretty much the same, too. Ornate Victorian homes crowd the streets and avenues. Some cared for, some not.

So, I'll admit, I knew he was talking about Orchard Ridge, but I wanted to see what'd he say.

"Yes, it reminds me of Orchard Ridge, if that's what you're asking. But, to be honest, it reminds me of a lot of places I've lived. One small town is really no different from the next, I suppose."

I'm not sure how to respond to this. I'll admit it piques my interest, which kind of pisses me off because I don't want to be interested in the old man. But then I remember my dad's letter, which I've been carrying around in my wallet. I wish that I could hold it right now, rub it between my fingers like a talisman, just to give me a little bit of strength because I need to do what my dad wanted to do himself. I need to ask the right questions, to find out all of the Wheres and the Whats and the Whys.

"So," I say, clearing my throat, warming up my nerves,

"where *have* you lived?"

"You mean, where did I go after I left your dad and his mom?"

This really takes me by surprise. So much so that I nearly trip over a heaving slab of sidewalk. "Sure. You can start there, I guess."

John doesn't look at me as he talks; instead, he just stares straight ahead. I suspect that looking at me reminds him too much of his son, as if time has stood still and has kept his son preserved until his return, like Han Solo frozen in carbonite. Finally, he says, "For a long time, I just kind of traveled around, which was easy in my line of work."

"And what was your 'line of work'?" I won't lie. An image of him as a hit man flashes through my mind. I see him hiding in a black car, tinted windows and all, outside some poor guy's house, shoving a clip into a revolver and waiting for just the right moment to fire away before speeding off into the night.

"Carpentry, mostly," he says, kicking aside a stone. "But I'm really a jack of all trades, so it was easy for me to pick up work here and there. Especially since I never charged quite as much as most other guys."

"Sounds like a great business model," I say with evident sarcasm.

"Well, I never really cared about making a lot of money. I just cared about getting by, I suppose."

"So you'd just float from town to town like some gypsy carpenter and find random work?"

John almost laughs. "I guess you could say that.

Eventually, I did settle in one place."

"Where?" We're almost home, just a block or so away. Hayden is still in front of us, but he's talking to Louise, an elderly woman whose lawn he mows. I'm sure she's berating him for not cutting her grass in perfectly executed rows. Seriously. The woman clips her hedges with scissors, for God's sake.

"Pennsylvania. Amish country."

This, I definitely was not expecting. "*Amish* country? You're kidding me, right?"

"Honest to God," he says, holding up his right hand. "I'm a simple man, Parker. Believe it or not."

"Wait," I say, shaking my head in desperate need of clarification. "Did you live *with* the Amish? Like, without electricity and stuff?" I'm trying to picture him now in a straw hat and suspenders.

"No. I didn't actually live with them. Just near them. They were my neighbors is all."

So, we have some of the What and the Where out of the way, but it's the Why that I'm really interested in now. And it's the Why that my dad would've wanted to know. But just as I'm finally working up the nerve to ask the old man about why he left, he suddenly doubles over.

"John?" I say, actually concerned. "Are you okay?"

He's bent over, clutching his knees, breathing loudly. "Yeah," he manages to say between rattling breaths. "Just got...a little lightheaded, I guess."

"What's wrong?" Hayden is beside us now. He's left Louise at her fence, gawking at us.

John straightens his back and waves his hand at Hayden. "I'm all right."

Hayden grips John's arm and leads him back to our house. "Don't worry," he says, "I gotcha."

I follow them for a few minutes until I remember what my mom said to me the other day: *I want you to be nicer. I want you to be you.* I step to the other side of the old man and help him along. It's the first time that I've really touched him since we shook hands. His arm — I don't know why — feels a lot frailer than I expected, mostly skin and bone.

When my mom sees us walking John up the driveway, she rushes out of the house. "What happened?" she cries, replacing me by his side. For a brief second, I wonder if she thinks that I'm responsible for this.

"Oh, like I told Parker, I just got a little lightheaded. Don't worry too much about it, Grace. Really. I'm fine."

I watch the three of them walk into the house and realize that I didn't get to ask the most important question: Why?

CHAPTER 18

Still No Answer

So, it's officially summer. *Finally*. No more exams. No more projects. The Evolution of Things was a success, by the way, even when you consider the fact that a rogue first grader decided that it might be a good idea to try and ride the pterodactyl that Sarah and I had made. Needless to say, our pterodactyl did not survive. Both of his wings snapped off as soon as the little bastard jumped on his back. The scene definitely made me wonder about our current theories regarding dinosaur extinction. Screw climate shifts and giant asteroids. I bet it was just a bunch of delinquent six and seven-year-old brats that snuck out of their caves and killed them off with their high-pitched screams, sticky fingers, and refusal to follow even the simplest of directions, like *Please don't touch the dinosaur.*

Anyway, nothing beats the sense of freedom you get when you walk out of school for the last time before summer vacation, all those endless days stretching out in front of you, nothing but fun as far as the eye can see.

But this is the first summer without Dad. Because he was an English professor, he had the summers off with us, which meant that we could go fishing or canoeing or hiking whenever we wanted. Summer was *our* time. Now, I kind of feel like it just yawns before us, like it will be nothing but slow and sluggish without Dad to keep us constantly entertained. Even his canoe, the one he'd had since he was my age, is still covered with its winter tarp. We would have had it in the water by now, paddling our way across the glassy surface of Haywood Lake or down the rippling waves of the Glendale River.

The kayak he died in? It's not here. My mom didn't want it back.

A few of the guys, Noah and Dante and Victor, got a job picking berries at Tanner's Farm. It's a shitty job, but at least it means that they'll pretty much have the same hours as I do, working early in the morning. Evenings will be ours then. However, my mom has already warned me that the family dinner rule will still be in effect.

Since Murphy has been doing such a great job at The Mill, Mom has decided to give her morning hours on a rotating schedule with Madge. I'm kind of bummed that I won't get to work much with Charlie, but Murphy and I are becoming fast friends. And Madge? Well, you know, it's *Madge*.

Because mornings are crazy at the coffeehouse and because Murphy hasn't quite mastered the espresso machine, she takes the orders and dishes up the pastries and muffins while I handle the coffee. It's a good system. Since she's so small, we never get in each other's way. I can pretty much pass people their lattes right over her head.

This morning, Sarah stops in. She's dressed in jean shorts that are so short, the white pockets poke out from under them. She's also got on a tank top that's kind of big and breezy but still manages to show off her figure, especially when she's standing in the light, which she's doing right now, making it impossible not to stare at her.

"Hey, Parker," she says, walking up to the counter.

"Hey." I try to avert my eyes, focus on something else. Act cool. But my eyes won't obey me. They are stuck on Sarah, like two magnets.

Sarah turns to Murphy. "Hi, Murphy."

"Hi. You want an iced coffee?"

"Yes! Please. It's so freaking hot out, I'm literally melting."

"Shot of vanilla?" Murphy asks, loading a clear plastic cup with ice.

"Better not. I don't need the extra calories." She's looking past us now and at her reflection in the mirror that hangs behind the counter. She even turns sideways, her hands pressed against her stomach, her shoulders kind of thrown back.

Murphy rolls her eyes and hands Sarah her coffee. "You can't be serious."

"Hey," Sarah says as she pushes a straw through the lid of her cup, "it's summer. Have to keep it slim, right?"

"Jesus Christ," Murphy mumbles to herself.

Before she walks out, Sarah turns around and says, "Victor's dad is out of town, so he's having a party in the field behind his house tomorrow night."

"Really? I didn't know that," I say, suddenly feeling like I've been left out of the loop.

"He just decided. I got the text before I walked in here. You should come."

"Sure. Maybe," I say. "Did Victor threaten his dad again or something?"

"I have no idea. Probably."

As much as Victor despises his father, he has absolutely no problem taking advantage of him. Then again, maybe it's easier taking advantage of people you don't like. I mean, think about it: What's there to lose? There's nothing to be sacrificed. No relationship to be flushed down the toilet. Victor probably just believes that his father owes him something, even if it is just a few beers or a place to throw a party. He'll take whatever he can get.

"You should come, too, Murphy," Sarah says without actually making eye contact because she's too preoccupied with her phone, running her thumb up and down its screen.

Murphy, who looks less than thrilled by the invitation, says, "A field party at Victor's house? How can I resist?"

"Cool," says Sarah, stuffing her phone in her back pocket before walking out the door. I watch her as she stands on the sidewalk for a moment, stopping to check her phone again. She smiles at something, and I have to wonder if she's read another message from Victor.

"You like her," Murphy says, and I can't help but notice that it sounds more like an accusation than an observation.

"No, I don't," I lie, feeling my neck and face warming to a soft red glow.

"Yes. You do." She crosses her arms. She looks disappointed. Mad, even. I can see her brown eyes narrowing into little, accusatory crescents.

"It wouldn't even matter if I did, anyway. She likes Victor, and he likes her. Sort of."

Murphy smirks. Sometimes I feel like that crooked smile is permanently carved into her tiny face. "What? Are you following some sort of bro code or something?"

"Sure. Yeah. I guess." I am in very dangerous territory here. My — I don't even know what to call it — *infatuation* with Sarah has been under lock and key, stored safely in a box, left to collect dust. But Murphy has found the key and is threatening to unlock my secret.

Luckily, she calms my nerves. "Don't worry. I won't say anything. It's really none of my business, anyway."

"Thanks," I say, relieved.

"Only, I don't know why you'd ever want someone so — how shall I say this? — desperate. Or pathetic. Maybe that's the better word." Murphy is stacking some mugs on the counter with so much force that a few white ceramic shards fall to the floor.

"What do you mean?" I ask, half-wondering if I should go to the mugs' rescue.

She turns around and says, "Don't get me wrong. I think Sarah is nice and all, but I can't stand girls who just make themselves so available all the time to douchebags like Victor."

I search for the right thing to say here, but all I can come up with is "Well, Victor isn't a *complete* douche."

"Yeah," she rolls her eyes, "okay."

I walk home with a mind full of fog because I'm still not sure who Murphy's more annoyed with: Victor? Sarah? Me? I hate feeling like there's someone out there in the world who's angry with me. It makes me feel trapped, like I'm their prisoner, locked up indefinitely for a crime that I'm not entirely convinced I've committed.

So I text her. U in tmrw? I figure that she'll know that I'm talking about Victor's party.

She answers almost immediately. Sure.

Great, I text back.

Tonight, it's just going to be Hayden, John, and me. My mom is attending a town board meeting because apparently someone wants to open a Dunkin' Donuts on the corner of Main Street and Route 71, which has Mom completely pissed off and, as she says, "Ready to spit bricks." The Mill is our only source of income now, and we can't afford to lose any customers.

Anyway, what this really means is that we'll be alone with the old man.

When I walk into the kitchen, John is cooking dinner again. "It's not soup again, is it?" I ask.

"No. Shrimp and risotto."

"Oh," I say, a bit shocked. The aromas of browned butter and lemon hit my nose, and my mouth starts to water.

"Sounds good, actually."

"Here," John says, handing me a wooden spoon, his hand shaking. "Can you stir the risotto for a bit?"

I take the spoon and stir the rice around the pan, not really paying much attention to what I'm doing. "Pour some more broth in there, would you?" he says, turning his back to me and pulling some pills from his pocket before filling his glass with water from the faucet. I do as I'm told and keep stirring.

"What're those pills for?" I ask.

"Nothing. Just vitamins is all."

I stop stirring the risotto. "Do you always carry vitamins around in your pocket?"

"Keep stirring," he says.

"Sorry."

John sits down at the table and gulps down his pills.

I lift the spoon from the rice, but he nods at the pan, reminding me that I must keep stirring. "Sorry. This rice is a little high maintenance."

"I suppose you're right. But it's worth it." I notice that he's rubbing his stomach, kind of in a circular motion.

"Your stomach bothering you?"

"Nah. Just hungry." Then he says, "I never cooked much when your father was young. His mother did most of the cooking. Guess that's just how it was back then."

"But then you were on your own, so you had to cook."

John's shoulders sink a little. "I learned to cook, yes. Over the years. I enjoy it now. It relaxes me. Everyone needs something to relax, don't you think?"

"Sure. I guess." I wonder where Hayden is because I suddenly feel like I need him here. You know, as a buffer.

"Go ahead and add the shrimp," he says, pointing at the bowl full of shrimp he's already seasoned. While I'm stirring again, he starts reminiscing. "When your dad was a boy, I used to take him fishing. We'd fish for hours. Spend entire afternoons just casting in our lines, waiting for a bite, tossing most of the fish we caught back in. Sometimes we'd talk; other times, we'd just...listen. Anyway, that's what I did to relax. Back then.

"So," John continues, clearing his throat, "did your dad still fish much? Did he ever take you and Hayden?"

Even though it probably shouldn't, this takes me by surprise. I have been so hell-bent on finding out answers for myself — and for Dad — that I have completely ignored the fact that John probably has quite a few questions of his own. And, despite my intention to be nothing but angry with him, I suddenly feel sorry for him for not really knowing my dad. His son. Actually, my dad always used to say that regret leaves the deepest scars. "You can't see them, Parker," he'd say, "but they're long and deep and never really fade." So, like a sudden change in the weather triggers the pain of an old injury, I suspect that my questions must do the same for John.

Still, it's not enough to stop me, which makes me ignore his question and ask another one of my own. "Did you ever wonder...I mean...did you ever think about — "

"Jackie?" he interrupts. "Of course. All the time. Leaving doesn't mean forgetting, Parker."

"I'm not so sure my dad would agree with that."

John looks at me with an expression that I can't quite figure out. It's kind of a muddled composition of shame and sadness and loneliness. "I suppose you're probably right," he admits.

Then, finally, I ask the question that's been knocking at the chambers of my heart since the day he arrived. "Why then? Why'd you leave?"

The question hangs in the air like a spider dangling over our heads.

But just like the other day, the moment is hijacked. This time by Hayden, who comes running down the stairs and into the kitchen. "Smells awesome. I love shrimp," he says, peeking around me at the dish on the stove.

"Well, that's good to hear," the old man says. "I'm happy to oblige your taste buds."

John gets up to plate the risotto and shrimp, but not before giving me a quick, sideways glance. I can tell he's relieved. Still, he knows he owes me an answer. After all, he's had almost thirty years to come up with one.

CHAPTER 19

Cold Light

Murphy texted me for directions to Victor's party. I offered to drive out to Glendale and pick her up, but she said she wanted to drive herself. I worry that this is a sign that she's still annoyed with me somehow, but I try to push the thought aside. I want to have a good time tonight.

The last time Victor had a party in the field behind his dad's house, things got a little crazy. See, Victor plays both football and lacrosse, and the guys who play these sports tend to be anything but chill. Their idea of a good time is to be as loud as possible, as if having fun requires a certain amount of intensity, a primitive, chest-pounding posturing, like gorillas in the jungle. I hate to stereotype, but that's kind of what they are. Just can-smashing asshats. The more they drink, the louder and more aggressive they get. I mean, if it weren't illegal, I bet their coaches would love to put some beer in their cooler instead of water. They'd probably win more games, as long as they didn't pass out first.

I tend never to drink too much at Victor's parties, mostly because I feel like someone's got to be responsible. However, at the last field party, I drank enough so that I smelled like beer when I got home. It also didn't help that one of Victor's football buddies, a kid who goes by No Pain Lane, puked all over my sneakers. That was just a few months ago, right before Dad died, when it was unusually warm out in early March. I'd come home to find my dad waiting for me in the kitchen. He was a little strung out on grading midterm papers, but not so much so that he couldn't tell that I'd been drinking.

"Parker," he said, tossing his pencil on the table. (He never used a red pen to grade. He thought it was too intimidating, like someone bled all over the papers.) "Were you drinking in that field behind Victor's father's house?"

"Uh...um," I stammered, wishing I'd remembered to take off my shoes before I came inside.

"You should know that Frank called. Said there were some kids partying out there." Frank is the town sheriff. He's skinny and short and looks like he's twelve. Not very threatening for a cop.

"Okay," I said, because I couldn't think of anything else, although I was wondering why the sheriff hadn't just broken up the party. He was probably too scared to try and disperse us himself.

"I hope that's not your puke I smell." Dad picked up his pencil and started reading another paper.

113

I looked down at my sneakers. "No. It's not."

"Just be careful, Parker. We trust you. Don't ruin that, okay?"

"I won't," I said. And I'd meant it.

When I get to Victor's dad's house, there are already a ton of cars and trucks lining the edge of the road, some of them leaning so far over, I think they might tip over into the ditch. I walk down the road, toward the driveway, remembering that I hate walking into a party by myself. It makes me feel just a little bit pathetic. Thankfully, I find Noah, Dante, and the twins right away; and, thankfully, they had the forethought to bring some lawn chairs. "My mom's always got these in the back of her car. Mandatory accessories of the soccer mom," Dante tells us.

"Just don't spill any beer on them." It's Roman, Dante's older brother.

"Roman. Hey," I say. "I didn't know you were home." We shake hands, very formally.

"Just for the weekend. I've got an internship in New York. I'm heading back early Monday morning."

Behind him, I see Charlie walking toward us, beer in hand.

"What're you doing here?" I ask.

"What?" Charlie says. "And miss a good, old fashioned field party?"

"What Parker means to say," Noah chimes in, "is that you seem a little beyond the field party scene."

Roman swings an arm over Charlie's shoulder. "C'mon.

This is vintage Haywood."

"Yeah," Charlie agrees. "Totally old school. Besides, what the hell else is there to do around here on a Saturday night?"

"Good point," Dante says.

"You boys have fun," Roman says before he and Charlie leave our circle.

I notice Dante is drinking a bottle of water. "Are you DD tonight?"

He looks forlornly at his water. "Sadly, yes. I've been reduced to chauffeuring the Chosen One." He's referring to Roman, of course. See, Dante has spent his entire life traipsing around in the rather large and looming shadow of his older brother. It's always been about Roman, the Homecoming King; Roman, the Soccer Star; Roman, the Law Student at Columbia. Dante, though, is just a better *person* than his brother. Kindness, I'm learning, is usually considered a distant third behind looks and athleticism. I have to wonder if Dante will ever get over his inferiority complex. I hope he does.

It's barely dark, and Victor is already wasted. He comes around and collects money so that he can order pizza. "We're ordering from Orazio's."

"Dude, come *on*," Tony protests. "You know their pizza sucks ass. The last time we ordered from there, the pizza wasn't even cooked in the middle. And it looked like someone had thrown an entire bucket of onions on it."

"Yeah, but their side orders are awesome," Victor says as he grabs Tony by the shoulders and gives him a little shake. He nearly trips over himself when he walks away, regaining his balance just before almost falling face-first into the keg.

"What's that supposed to mean?" I ask, but I'm actually a little preoccupied. Murphy hasn't shown up yet, which makes me wonder if she's still coming. I keep looking at the driveway hoping to see a tiny shadow heading my way.

Dante says, "Apparently, people are dealing out of Orazio's."

"Seriously?" Gabe asks.

"Supposedly," says Noah. "The delivery guys just stash it in the pizza boxes. Pretty genius, actually."

I shake my head. "Victor's stupid, man."

"And you're just now realizing this?" Noah asks, a smirk on his face.

We all sort of chuckle at this, but we all know it's not really funny. If drinking or smoking is the occasional pastime for us, it's becoming a habit of Victor's. In some ways, I think Victor is the saddest member of the Dudes with Dead Dads Club. Sure, our dads are dead; but when they were alive, they loved us, and we knew that. Victor is just cursed with a dad who chooses to drift in and out of his life in a very unpredictable pattern. If I were to make a line graph of his father's appearances, it would look like a mountain range, rising and falling, with more valleys than peaks.

After about another hour or so, I spot Sarah. She's sitting on a plastic crate near the edge of the field, where the yard meets the taller, unmowed grass. "Hey!" she says when she sees me walking toward her.

"Hi," I say back, sitting in the grass. It's already a little damp, but I don't care.

"You wanna sit up here? I can make room." She scoots over a little on the crate, offering me a corner of it, which I accept. The best part is that she immediately leans against me. Her hair, which is loose, tickles the back of my neck. I can even smell her shampoo, which smells like vanilla and green apples and something else. The woods maybe. Or spring. Whatever it is, it's amazing. I'm tempted to lean right into her and just breathe her in.

"So," she says, "how's John?"

"Fine, I guess."

"He seems like a nice guy."

"Yeah." But I don't want to talk about John. I want to hold her hand. I want to feel her fingers woven with my own.

Victor and one of his football buddies come running past us, yelling and grabbing at each other until they are both rolling around on the ground. "What a disaster this night is going to be," I hear Sarah mutter to herself.

"Why do you even like him, anyway?" I blurt out before I even know what I'm saying.

Sarah shifts a little on the crate so that she can see my face, if only in her periphery. "He's your friend, Parker," she says in a tone that makes me wonder if she knows how I feel about her.

I'm nervous now and in desperate need of some serious backpedaling. "No, I know. I just mean...I just meant — "

"It's okay," Sarah interrupts. "I know. I know you guys all think I'm pretty stupid for hanging out with Victor, like I'm some sort of glutton for punishment. Or some ho-bag with no self-respect. But you don't know him like I do. And, besides, he's been through a lot."

Words catch and burn in my throat, like shards of glass. There is so much I want to say, so much I want to tell her. "I just think you can do better. That's all I'm saying."

"Oh yeah? And who do you have in mind?"

I move my hand so that our fingers are touching, but just barely. She tilts her head back so that it's resting on my shoulder, and then she turns it slightly so that I can feel her warm breath against my neck. Here we are, at the edge of the yard, at the edge of the party, at the edge of everything. If I'm going to make a move, it's now or never. *Kiss her*, I tell myself.

"Sarah!" A familiar voice finds us. It's Victor. He's stumbling toward us.

Sarah sighs. "I'm right here!" she calls back. But before she leaves me to go to Victor, she whispers into my ear, "Thanks, Parker."

"For what?"

"For...saying what you said."

I sit on the crate for a while, just watching the fireflies blinking on and off in the field. "Cold light," my dad told me once when we were camping. "It's called bioluminescence, a chemical reaction. It's bright, but it doesn't produce any heat." I wonder if that's what I am to Sarah. Just cold light.

I look at my phone. It's ten o'clock. I wander back over to Dante and the others who are still pretty much where I left them, except that there's a fire now in the center of their misshapen circle, and they are all staring at it as if hypnotized by the lapping flames. "Did Murphy ever show up?" I ask, barely breaking their trance.

Tony, with his eyes still on the fire, "Yeah. She was here, looking for you."

"Well, where is she now?"

"I told her that you were over there talking to Sarah. She started to walk over there, but then she disappeared, I guess," Noah tells me.

"Why would she leave?" I ask, mostly to myself.

There is a wave of shoulder shrugs that moves its way around the circle. It's not that they don't care; it's just that they really don't know. Gabe mumbles, "Women," and we all nod our heads in absolute agreement.

CHAPTER 20

Dad's House

When I get home, there's a note on my bed. I'm a little hesitant to read it, considering the last letter that I found there, but I snatch it up and read it, anyway. *Parker, I'm giving you the morning off tomorrow*, it declares in my mom's loopy handwriting. *You're spending the day with John.*

"Hell. No." It's late, but I don't care. I stomp down the hall to my mom and dad's room. The light's still on, but even if it weren't, the darkness wouldn't stop me. She can't do this to me. She can't. It's just too much. I grip the doorknob and open her door, not even bothering to knock first. "Mom," I say, holding up her note, "seriously?"

She puts down the book she's reading, pushing back the pages that are about to fall away from it, like dead leaves from a tree, and says, "Yes, Parker. Seriously."

"I don't understand why you keep pushing this on me." All those times Dad trusted her judgment, let her make the decisions, I wonder now if he ever had his doubts.

"Parker, you said you would try."

"I *am* trying," I tell her, slumping down on the bench at the end of their bed.

"I'll admit you're being nicer, but I wouldn't say you're really trying." She sits up and leans toward me. "I think that maybe...maybe your sadness is clouding your judgment a little."

"And yours isn't?"

Mom sighs and leans back against the metal frame of her bed. "I suppose that's fair." She looks past me. At what, I don't know. Then she says, "I just keep trying to do what your dad would do."

For a while, we just sit. Mom's got the windows open, so I can hear the crickets and the grasshoppers playing their music, like a wild symphony that seems never to rest and has a rhythm that's somehow both comforting and annoying.

This is also when I notice that Hayden's stuff is gone. His pillow, his blankets, everything. "Where's Hayden?" I ask.

"Sleeping. In his room."

"Oh. Well, that's good."

"Yes it is." Mom's eyebrows are perched high on her forehead. It's her *I-told-you-so* look.

"What? Don't tell me you're giving John credit for that."

"Why shouldn't I? Since he's been here, Hayden's better. He's happier. He likes talking to John about Dad."

Mom leans forward and reaches for my hand. "Maybe you should do the same."

"I am."

Mom tilts her head to the side. "No. You're more worried about figuring John out."

"Yeah? Maybe *you* should do the same," I say, flinging my mother's words back at her like a fistful of mud.

"What's there to figure out, Parker? He's ashamed of what he did. But, more than anything, he's just sad. Like the rest of us."

I don't like that my mom is lumping John in with all of us, as if his sadness were equal to our own. I want to say something to her about this, but then my eyes start to roam around the room. There are bits and pieces of my dad everywhere. The book that he was reading before he died is sitting on his nightstand, open to a page that's still waiting to be read. On his dresser sit his watch, some loose change, a few crumpled notes (probably reminders about meetings), a card that Mom gave him on their last anniversary. It's the saddest shrine in the world. I notice, too, that a pair of his jeans is still hanging on the back of their door. There's even a pair of his dirty socks lying like dead fish next to his side of the bed.

If I try hard enough, I can see him sitting next to my mom, looking at me with an expression that says, *Well*?

"Fine," I hear myself saying. "I'll spend the day with John."

The next morning, John, Hayden, and I all pile into John's truck. It's a small truck, just an old Ford Ranger, pocked with rust and loud as hell. It's the kind of truck that makes you want to sink into the seat as you drive around town, trying not to be seen because you are most definitely being heard.

"This is so cool," Hayden says. He's sitting in the middle and acting as if he's on some sort of amusement park ride. "Can I try shifting the gears?"

"I don't know," says the old man. "She can be a little temperamental."

"How hard can it be?" asks Hayden, crossing his arms.

John smiles, but he concentrates on the road. "S'pose it's not that hard. Let's just get out of town here, and then maybe I'll let you give it a try."

Out of town? I think. "Where're we going exactly?"

"You'll see." Suddenly, I feel like we're being kidnapped, taken against our will. I am, at least. Hayden is bouncing up and down, happy as ever, which makes me want to do nothing more than smack the hell out of him. It's like he's figured out how to keep his grief and his happiness completely separate, like they're oil and water; while I feel all shaken up, sadness and hope and every other emotion all mixed together, making me wonder if I'll ever feel purely happy again.

I crack the window and close my eyes, letting the cool wind whip against my face. I even manage to doze off for a while until I feel the truck jerk to the side. "What was that?" I say, alert now.

"Sorry," John says, "Deer."

"Oh." I rub my eyes and look around, and I'm surprised to discover that everything looks familiar.

"Hey! I know where we are!" shouts Hayden, his sudden

awareness matching my own.

We're in Orchard Ridge, where Mom and Dad grew up. "What're we doing here?" I ask, thoroughly confused.

"I thought you might like to see where your dad grew up," John says, turning down West Avenue.

"We've already seen it," I tell him. Every time we visit our grandparents — Mom's parents, I mean — we drive past it. And every time, Dad points it out. Well, *pointed* it out.

I wonder what it would be like to jump out of this truck. We can't be going that fast, can we? How bad could it hurt? I've seen enough movies, watched enough guys jump out of trucks or trains and tumble down steep, stone-covered hills without so much as a scratch to show for it. I could probably do it, right? Just tuck and roll. I grip the handle with my sweaty hand. I should do it. I should just jump.

"Yeah," Hayden says, disappointment lacing his words. "Dad showed it to us. Lots of times."

John takes a quick right down Prospect Street. "But did you ever get to see the inside?"

"No way!" Hayden yells. "Really? But how? Do you still have a key? Are we breaking in?"

When John pulls into the driveway, I notice that there's a sign in the front lawn: FOR SALE BY OWNER.

John says, "I drove through here on my way to Haywood and saw that the house was for sale. So, I called the owner the other day and asked if we could see it. Of course, I did have to pretend that I was an interested buyer."

Hayden nods with approval. "Smooth move, dude."

We climb out of the truck, and I'm feeling sick. Sick, but

also — and I hate to admit this — a little curious. I have always wondered about this place. When I was younger, I used to love to hear stories about my parents' childhood, what they did, who their friends were. With Mom, it was easy because her parents still live in the same house; they've been there for over forty years. I didn't need much of an imagination to picture my mom when she was younger running around her yard or sneaking out of the house through the basement window. But with Dad, it was different. I had to fill in the blanks. In some ways, it was more fun that way. It allowed for a little harmless hyperbole, for both Dad and for me.

A woman, probably in her mid-thirties, greets us at the door. John, after misleading her on the phone, explains now that he used to live here with his family and that he was just hoping to show his grandsons the house. The woman is a little reluctant and obviously disappointed. Still, she swings the door open and lets us in.

The house is bigger than I expected. From the outside, it looks quite small. A bungalow, I think they call it. There are two oak columns that serve as an entryway into the living room, which has a large brick fireplace that's flanked by two built-in bookshelves. John reaches out and touches one of the columns. He even rubs his hand up and down the edge of it.

"Did you build these?" asks Hayden, touching the other one.

"No. Just refinished them. With your dad. They'd been covered in layers of paint. We spent an entire summer stripping them, sanding them, and then staining them. Labor of love, I guess you could say."

When John and Hayden walk into the living room to check out the fireplace, I touch one of the columns, too, and I feel something move through me like an electric shock. At home, I'm around all of Dad's things; but it's different, being here. I want to see more, touch everything. I walk into the living room where John and Hayden are and check out the shelves. Right now, they're crowded with a bunch of bins filled with toys and DVDs and video games, so I try to imagine them as they would have been when Dad was here: stuffed with nothing but books.

John, as if reading my mind, says, "These shelves nearly collapsed with all the books your dad used to pile on them. My *God*, he was a reader.

"And you see those bricks right up here?" he says, pointing to the top left corner of the fireplace. "We replaced those. In fact, we wrote our initials on the back of one of the bricks. It was your dad's idea. He kind of liked to leave his mark on things."

We spend another hour inside the house. The owner, Carla, warms up to us. She even offers to make us lunch, which we accept. It seems she likes hearing about the house, too. "Stories sell houses. So whatever you can tell me will only help my cause."

While she makes us turkey sandwiches and lemonade, we explore the second floor. When John points out what used to be Dad's room, all three of us walk in, one after the other. The room, thankfully, is still a boy's room. A basketball hoop hangs from the back of the door; a box full of Nerf guns sits in the corner; and rusty, old road signs hang on the walls, shouting words at us like STOP and DEAD END. I wonder if these signs may have a deeper warning and think about saying so, but then I see Hayden, and the thoughts scurry away just as fast as they appeared. Tears are spilling from his eyes, rolling slowly down his cheeks. I put my arm around him, and he wraps his arms around my waist and leans his head against the side of my ribs. Then, I feel something on my shoulder. It's John's hand. For a long time, we just stand in my dad's childhood room, breathing in what little of him might be left here.

"I wonder...." John says, walking toward the closet. He opens the door and gently pushes back the clothes that are hanging in his way. He smiles to himself. "C'mere. I want to show you something."

We walk over to the closet to see what it is that John's pointing at. The inside of it is covered with writing. Poems, quotes, random doodles. My dad's version of hieroglyphics. Unable to resist, I step inside of the closet and just start reading. I feel like an archeologist making a discovery, excited and a little bit frightened by what I might find. Near the doorframe, there's a poem written in thick black ink. I recognize the poem right away, too. It's a Wendell Berry poem, "The Peace of Wild Things," one of Dad's favorites.

"Look," I tell Hayden and John, moving over so they can read it, too.

I reach out and touch the words as we read them, silently. *When despair for the world grows in me*...but I can't read the rest because I feel something inside of me begin to crack. And then I hear John whisper the final line, "I rest in the grace of the world, and am free."

For a long while, none of us says anything. I think we are too afraid that something might break inside of us if we do. Then John reaches out and touches the words just as I did a moment ago, running his fingers across them, slowly and deliberately. They pause at the same line my eyes have been lingering over for too long.

Probably to save us from this torturous silence, John clears his throat and says, "I caught him writing this here one night. I'd just come back after being gone for a few days. His mother and I had had a fight, so I'd taken off even though I'd promised I'd take him fishing. I didn't yell at him. Figured I didn't really have a right to, after what I'd done, breaking my promise. The next morning I found a copy of a Wendell Berry book on the seat of my truck. He'd bought it for me for my birthday. I'd actually forgotten that it was my birthday, but he hadn't. I don't think I ever even thanked him for it."

"Why would he write this on the wall, though? In his closet? It's...kinda weird," Hayden says, his voice cracking a little.

"He used to read in here, when he was a boy. Used to drag all of his blankets and books in here with him. Sometimes he'd even sleep in here. Feels pretty small now, doesn't it?"

"Well, there *are* three of us in here, so...." Hayden says, beginning to regain himself.

John and Hayden leave the room and go back downstairs where Carla is waiting to serve us lunch. On their way down, I hear Hayden say, "So how old was he when he wrote that?"

"Oh," John says, "probably around your age. Eleven or

twelve."

"He read poetry, even back then? Man, he'd never survive middle school these days."

I can't move. Not just yet. I trace the letters once more with my finger, following the up and down rhythm of my father's hand; and for too long I stare at the same line, the one that makes my heart want to leap out of my chest.

I come into the presence of still water.

CHAPTER 21

Finding Out Why

The drive home is quiet. I think we are all too focused on our thoughts. It's strange, visiting my dad's past without him there to navigate it. Yes, John was there; but perspective is everything, you know?

Hayden actually falls asleep, and I let him rest his head on my shoulder. When we get home, Mom is waiting for us. I think she knew all along where we were going by the way she's looking at me. "Well?" she asks, a little scared and tugging on Dad's wedding ring that still hangs around her neck.

"It was...good," I say. "And weird."

Mom hugs me and whispers, "Thank you." When she pulls away from me, she sniffs and wipes her eyes. "Grilled hot dogs for dinner?"

"You mean grilled wieners?" Hayden laughs and then

attempts to wink, which he's incapable of doing. His face just won't let him.

"Sure," Mom says, rolling her eyes. "Why do all boys find wieners, farts, and poop to be so funny?"

"Because," I say, giving Hayden a fist bump, "they are."

We eat dinner outside. Hayden tells Mom all about Carla, how she seemed kind of mean at first but then made lunch for us and told us all about her divorce and her cheating husband and that's why she's selling the house so she can stick it to him. "Sounds like an open book, this Carla," Mom remarks, her eyebrows raised.

"She was," John agrees, "but I'm glad she agreed to let us take a look around."

"Me, too," I say, and I mean it. I really do.

When we finish dinner, Mom offers to take us all out for ice cream, but only Hayden wants to go. After they leave, John and I clean up the dishes. "I know," John says, washing the salad bowl, "that you still have some questions. One in particular."

I take the bowl from him and give it a once-over with the towel. "Yeah?"

"You want to know why I left your dad and your grandmother."

I shake my head, but I don't say anything because I want to stay out of the way, let him keep talking.

"The truth is, Parker, I don't think why I left matters very much. It's just the What that counts. It's the What that everybody sees and feels. The Why never usually makes anybody *feel* better. They think it will, but it never does." He stops, stares out the window. I'm afraid that this is all I'm going to get, which isn't very much. It feels mostly like a lecture, one meant to prepare for the fact that he *isn't* going to tell me. But then he says, "When Jackie's mother, your grandmother, and I got married, we were barely out of high school. We'd been dating for just a little while when she got pregnant, and I thought the only right thing to do was to marry her. So, that's what I did. We were eighteen when your dad was born. Just kids. We barely knew ourselves, let alone each other. We discovered over the years that we didn't like each other very much. Or, to put it nicely, that we didn't have much in common.

"Oh, don't get me wrong, there were some good times along the way. Mostly because of Jackie, though. But those good times became fewer and fewer until they dwindled to none at all, it seemed. She wasn't happy; I wasn't happy. I can't imagine your dad was very happy, either." He stops again, fixes his eyes on me. I think he wants me to agree with him, to share in the assumption that no, Dad wasn't happy back then, which might give the old man a pass, temper his guilt a little. But I don't say anything. I just wait for him to keep going because I feel like we're finally building toward the climax here.

"So," he says, apparently getting the hint, "I started accepting jobs that took me away from home. Sometimes for just a few days; sometimes for weeks on end. Staying away was easier. Until, one day, it just became the answer, I guess."

For a moment, I imagine my dad sitting by the window of his room, waiting until he couldn't wait any longer, until he grew tired of waiting. I imagine him dragging himself to his closet, closing himself in, writing words on the wall, eventually emerging from his cocoon wearing a sad look that I'm not sure I'd recognize.

Finally, I say, "So you just went to work one day and never came back."

"Yes."

"No letter or anything? Just...left?"

"Yes."

"Huh" is all I can manage to say.

John sits down, takes a few pills from his pocket and swallows them, not even bothering to get a glass of water. I sit down, too, and try to think of something to say, but the words won't come. "You look...disappointed," John says, resting his hands on the table.

"No," I answer. "Why would I be disappointed?"

"You were expecting a different explanation, I suspect."

I think about this for a moment. "Honestly? Yeah. I think I was. I don't know *what*, but something a little more — I don't know — dramatic, I guess." I'm trying to conjure an image, a clear picture of what I'd thought I'd find out, but I'm realizing now that I never really had one. I only ever felt as if whatever John did — whatever made him want to leave my dad — it had to be nothing short of earth shattering, which is why I'm not sure I one hundred percent believe him.

John rests his elbows on the table and leans toward me. "Let me ask you something."

"What?"

"What's heavier: a two-thousand-pound rock or one ton

of gravel?"

He's seriously setting me up for some lame-ass riddle right now? I think, but I decide to play along and offer him the obvious answer. "They weigh the same," I say, leaning back in my chair.

"Exactly."

"What's your point?" I ask, feeling a little toyed with now.

"It means," John says, "that all the little things eventually add up until they weigh the same as one major screw up."

"Like an affair or something?"

"Right."

"Which you didn't have?"

"No."

"And you don't think just up and leaving was a 'major screw up'?" I ask. Treading lightly at this point doesn't seem like much of an option.

John stands up and rubs at his stomach. "Well, I guess it'd be fair to say that I dropped a mighty big rock onto a big pile of gravel."

"I guess."

"Parker," he says, leaning against the counter, "I don't know what else to say. I have no excuse, no reasons other than the ones I gave you. I'm telling you what I'd tell your dad. If he were here. The truth of the matter is that sometimes ...sometimes people just *leave*."

"Yeah," I say, but I'm not thinking of John. I'm thinking about my dad. "I guess sometimes they do." Disappearing? Dying? What's it matter when the end result is the same?

You're just left behind, floundering in a world that's suddenly and absolutely minus one.

Then, another thought occurs to me. "You could've just gotten divorced," I offer, as if the suggestion isn't several decades too late. "You could've stuck around. At least been one of those weekend dads. It would have been better than nothing."

John shuffles to the dishwasher and turns it on. "I thought about that. I really did. But, somehow, I thought Jackie would be better off. I'd been gone so much, I thought he'd already begun to hate me."

Hate was never a word I associated with my dad. He was incapable of it. He could get angry, yes, but even that was fleeting. So I say what I think my dad would want me to say: "I think he probably just missed you."

"Well," John whispers, "I missed him, too." He turns away from me and says, "You know, I kept tabs on him for a while, just through some people from Orchard Ridge. Guys I worked with mostly. I knew he'd married Grace."

"You never thought about contacting him?"

"Sure I did. But the longer you wait, the harder it is to figure out how to do that. The distance grows until it seems like it's just too much to cross."

"My dad didn't think so."

"I guess he didn't, did he?"

Of course, I could also argue that his death created even more distance. The insurmountable kind. The forever kind. But right now, I'm not entirely convinced of that. Sitting here, across the table from John, my dad's long-lost father, I think that maybe Dad's found a way to keep himself close.

Still, I can't shake the feeling that maybe the old man isn't filling in all of the blanks, like he's tucked away some truth he's too afraid to tell.

CHAPTER 22

A Walk with Murphy

Despite the fact that I've finally started to bond a little with John, the next week is absolutely miserable because it's my dad's birthday. He would have been forty-seven. We decided yesterday that we would all visit the cemetery together, place new flowers by Dad's headstone, clear away any debris that's gathered at the foot of it because, truthfully, there's nothing like a few brittle leaves and drooping flowers to make the dead seem, well, *more* dead.

    This morning, before we left for the cemetery, Mom baked Dad's favorite cake: chocolate with sticky coconut frosting. Every year, a few days before his birthday, she would ask him what kind of cake he wanted, and he always said the same thing: "You know. The chocolate one with all that gooey coconut and pecan frosting." And, because no one else in the family really likes coconut, he'd pretty much eat the entire thing himself. For breakfast and dessert. Anyway, seeing her in the kitchen, slowly stirring all that shredded coconut into the bowl, I was suddenly afraid that she actually wanted to *celebrate* his birthday, that she was going to make us wear stupid party hats and sing "Happy Birthday" or something equally sad and pathetic.

Thankfully, this does not happen. We do bring the cake, flowers, a basket, and some gloves to the cemetery, though. John and Hayden pull out the dead flowers and throw them in the basket; and Mom and I place the fresh flowers, big, bushy hydrangea blossoms, in the copper vase that's permanently affixed to the base of the headstone. Then, Mom just sits and talks to Dad as if he can answer her, as if she's having a real, extremely ordinary conversation with her husband on a real, extremely ordinary day. I can't do that. To be honest, I can barely stand to look at his name, which is glaring mercilessly at me with its hard, beveled edges.

This is also the first time that John has been here. With us, anyway. I suspect that he's been here before, alone. I wonder if he talked to my dad when he was here, if he knelt down and touched the fresh grass and cursed himself or God or fate or whatever else he could think of for being too late. Today, he's just quiet. I bet he figures that it's best to let Mom speak for all of us.

Just a little way down the hill, I see Noah. His dad is buried here, too. He sees me and waves, which I take as an invitation to walk over there. When I get near him, he says, "Fancy meeting you here."

"Yeah, well. It's my dad's birthday, so...."

"Right." Noah actually visits his father's grave with some frequency. I think other than the shed, this is probably the only place that gives him some sense of peace. He places a stone on top of his father's grave, and it immediately catches the light, sparkling like a jewel. "It gets easier, you know. Being here."

I don't say anything, but I know he doesn't expect me to. He understands that I'm still in the phase where nothing feels easy and everything feels labored and treacherous, especially today, as if I'm trying to swim against a hard, relentless current.

Noah looks over at my family. "Things better with — "

"My grandfather?"

"Ah," he smirks, "so we've graduated to calling him that now, huh?"

"Not to his face."

"Well. Progress," he nods.

"I guess."

Noah walks me back to my family, but before he leaves, he says, "You working tomorrow morning?"

"Nope. Tonight."

"Really?" he asks, surprised, his eyes landing on my family, as if to say, *What about them?*

"Yeah." Honestly, I *have* to work today. Mom had given me the day off, wanting us all to be together, but I told her that I thought that that was a bad idea. What would we do? Sit around and play a game called *Who's Sadder*? It would be pointless because I already know who'd win: all of us. In the sport of sadness, we're all champions.

"All right. Maybe we'll come by later then," Noah says before he turns to go.

"Okay. Later."

It's Open Mic Night at The Mill, so we're more swamped than usual. Every third Friday of every month is Open Mic Night, a tradition started by none other than Dr. Jack Warren, Professor of Poetry, Maestro of Metaphors, Rhyme Master, and Rhythm Coach. He loved these nights; and he abhorred them, too. He loved when he'd successfully convince one of his shyer (but talented) students to read something, but he hated having to tolerate the occasional high school student who bogarted the mic for too long with poems that reeked of cliché.

Unfortunately, I think that tonight might just be one of those nights that would have driven my father mad because Katrina Cochran is here. Katrina — or Katt, as she prefers to be called now — is a self-proclaimed poet who wears black clothing with silver studs on it; dyes her short, spiky hair about once a week; trims her bulging eyes in dark makeup; and spends the majority of her days sulking about something and then writing it down in a black notebook that she clutches to her chest as if it were armor. I can just hear my dad now: "My *God*, it's like Poe screwed an Anime character and made *that*!" Yes, the one thing that could turn my usually kind dad into a raging fool was really bad poetry.

Tonight, I'm actually working with Charlie and Murphy. It's the first real shift that I've had with Murphy since Victor's party, and we haven't talked much since then, so it's a little tense and awkward at first. Of course, Charlie doesn't help matters when he says, "Am I sensing a little sexual tension here, or is it just me?"

"It's just you," snaps Murphy.

"Shut up, Charlie," I tell him. I know he's joking, but I'm in no mood for it tonight.

Charlie says, "Sorry, man." Then, he leans a little closer and whispers, "Seriously, though, what is going on between you two? You've barely said two words to each other."

"I don't know," I say, and I really don't. Not really. "A little miscommunication, I guess."

"Whatever it is, you've got to make it right."

"Why me?"

"Because, Park, that's what you gotta do. It's always better to be the one who rights the wrong. Believe me."

"But what if I didn't even do anything wrong?" I protest.

Charlie doesn't say anything. He just stares at me with a look that says, *Yeah right*.

"Fine," I say, relenting. "I'll try."

Charlie stoops so that he's shorter than I am. "Do or do not. There is no —"

"Bro. Stop," I interrupt. "That's the worst Yoda impression I've ever heard."

"Lie you do," Charlie grumbles, still channeling his inner Yoda.

"For real. Stop. You sound like a broken cat."

He stands up and places his hand on this chest as if I've offended him. "Oh, now that's just cruel."

Murphy is at the front of the coffeehouse, keeping the aspiring poets under control. "Hey," I say to her. She's perched on a tall stool, so she's closer to eye-level.

"Hi," she says without looking at me. She's apparently studying the list of poets.

"So...um...sorry about the party. I didn't know you'd shown up. I waited for you, but after a while I kinda figured you weren't coming."

"Well, I was there."

"I know. I'm sorry. You didn't have to leave, though."

"I didn't want to interrupt you and Sarah."

This takes me by surprise, and I'm not really sure how to respond. "You wouldn't have been interrupting anything," I say, wishing that there *had* been something worth interrupting. "Anyway, I'm sorry." (Third time's a charm, right?)

"Fine."

Uh oh. While I admittedly don't have a lot of experience with women, I know that *Fine* just might be the kiss of death. I know that it usually means anything but fine, but I also don't know how to proceed from here. So out of nowhere, I blurt out, "Today's my dad's birthday." *What the hell am I doing?* I think. *Did I really just play the sympathy card?* I suddenly want to crawl under a rock.

It works, though, because Murphy finally looks at me. "I'm sorry," she says. "I didn't know."

I wave my hand at her. "That's all right," I tell her, sort of turning away because I can feel my skin burning, so much so that I'm convinced ugly, red splotches have crawled up my chest and neck.

"Hey," Katt calls from one of the chairs near the microphone. "We were supposed to start, like, ten minutes ago." She's wearing a plain black T-shirt, red shorts, and black Converse sneakers — or would they be called boots? — that go all the way up to her knees. She also has on these thick cuff bracelets that are encrusted in long, scary spikes.

Murphy jumps from her perch and sets the clipboard that bears the aspiring poets' names on the stool behind her. "We're almost ready," she tells Katt. Then she turns to me and says, "You've never really told me about your dad."

"That's true. I haven't," I admit. I shove my hands in my pockets, feel my shoulders rise, as if I'm just a marionette, my sadness pulling on the strings.

"Do you want to?" she asks, looking up at me. It's such a simple question, really, but the answer keeps changing. When it first happened, I didn't want to think about Dad at all, like pushing him out of my mind was a way of protecting myself. Then, I didn't want to share him with John, so I quietly refused to say anything, as if silence was a simple way to punish him.

And now?

Well, I think my answer surprises me as much as it does Murphy.

"Yeah. I think I do."

After I lock the door, Murphy and I just walk. It's a perfect summer night. Warm with a cool, generous breeze. Lots of people are out on their porches, rocking to the slow, lazy rhythms of summer; others are content to sit inside, their windows and lives open to the world. You can even hear the crickets and the peepers here in town. There's also the sound of kids playing in their yards, shouting at one another, fighting happily.

As we walk, we move in and out of the soft, silvery glow of the street lamps. Moths knock against the bright white lights, their papery wings reminding me of confetti floating through the air.

It's enough to make me want to write a poem. Almost.

We pass a fence that's lined with a bunch of rose bushes, their fat blossoms pushing past the white pickets, begging to be noticed. Even in the dark, you can tell they're red. A deep red, like scarlet or crimson or one of those fancier names for red when *red* feels just too generic. Murphy snaps one of the thorny stems and starts plucking the petals, one by one, dropping them along the way. "You need those to find your way back, or are you just rehearsing to play a flower girl in somebody's wedding?" I ask.

"No," she says, nudging me with her elbow. "I just like to keep my hands busy. I get nervous, otherwise."

"You? Nervous? About what?"

"So," Murphy starts, dropping another petal and ignoring my question. "What was he like, your dad?"

When someone you love dies, that is the most difficult question you can be asked: to describe the person you've lost to someone who's never met him. It seems nearly impossible; it's like trying to squeeze his soul, his very essence, into a tiny glass bottle, the kind that holds those fancy, tiny ships. See, while the question is too big and too overwhelming, it's the answer that feels beyond measure. It requires some serious whittling. So I say, "Ask something specific."

"Okay. What did he do?"

"He was an English professor."

"So I'm guessing that he loved to read?"

"Yes."

"Favorite book?"

"Wow."

"Too specific?"

I laugh. "No, no. It's just...he had lots of favorite books, so it's difficult to name just one."

"Just name one then. It doesn't have to be *the* one."

We walk a ways before I can answer. I'm trying to picture the books in my dad's office in the attic, the different towering obelisks, but it's taking me a little longer than I'd like to conjure up the titles. "Hmmm...well, poetry was his specialty. So, I'll pick a favorite poet. How's that?"

"Your call," Murphy says, batting away a rather aggressive moth.

"Robert Frost. And Wendell Berry."

"That's two," she says, walking backwards in front of me, still plucking petals.

"I know." I also know that I'm actually enjoying this conversation, that it feels good to talk about him.

"Did he have a nickname for you?"

"That's a weird question, and a total one-eighty in terms of subject matter."

Murphy points at me with what's left of the rose and smiles. "Classic avoidance. It must be a good one then. And totally embarrassing."

"No. I'm just wondering why you'd ask such a random

question."

"Aren't they all kind of random right now?"

"Good point."

"So? I'm still waiting." When I still don't answer, she says, "Oh, c'mon. All parents give their kids nicknames. It says something about the kid, but I think it says more about the parents."

"Gubby," I say, but only after we've stepped out of a cone of light. I don't want her to see my face turn mottled shades of red. Again.

"Gubby?" she repeats, smiling. "Oh, my God, that's really cute."

"I don't think I've ever heard you utter the word 'cute' before," I tease, moving a little closer to her.

"Don't tell anyone. I know spells, remember?" She waves her stem around as if it were a powerful, fearsome wand. It easily could be. It does have thorns, after all.

"Oh, that's right," I say as we brush shoulders. Well, as she brushes her shoulder against my arm.

"Any significance to this nickname?"

"Only that apparently I used to walk around the house when I was little singing, 'Everybody get your Gubby.' I have no idea what it means, but my dad just started calling me that. When I was still little, he'd pick me up and say, 'Well, I've got my Gubby! Where's yours?'" As I'm telling her this, I remember that I actually used to hate it when my dad called me Gubby in public. I used to give him the evil eye if he did, but it never stopped him, of course.

Murphy laughs. It sounds like a songbird, one that you'd

normally hear in the morning when the darkness is just starting to slink away. "Your dad sounds like he was a good guy."

"He was." I realize then that we've walked quite far from The Mill and that Murphy's car is still parked there. "We better turn around. It's getting kind of late."

Murphy pulls her phone from her back pocket and checks the time. "Oh, shit. Yeah, it is. My mom is going to freak out soon. I better send a preemptive text."

"I'll walk you back," I say because I'm not ready to stop talking.

"No, that's okay. Really."

"Please. Besides, my mom would kill me if she knew I let you walk back by yourself." I'd say that I'm just using this as an excuse, but it is most definitely true. She *would* kill me.

But Murphy's already moving away from me, fast, as if she has wings. I watch her as she flies through the dark, her blonde hair flapping behind her, until she turns around and yells, "G'night, *Gubby*."

And I can't help it. I smile.

CHAPTER 23

The Kiss

We haven't been to The Beehive since it officially opened, but Mom wants to go there tonight for dinner. I think she's starting to feel guilty because the meadery was Dad's project with Leo, and she loves Leo just as much as Dad did. Like lots of Dad's favorite places, though, it's difficult to spend too much time there without feeling like you're suffocating. Some people, I'm sure, feel the opposite. When someone you love dies, you may want to do nothing more than to wrap yourself up in what's left, make a cocoon out of it until you're ready to emerge, changed somehow. Healed, if you're the hopeful type.

Anyway, we decide to hold our breath and head to the meadery for dinner. They have a limited menu there. Snacks mostly. A variety of cheese and crackers, homemade breads, an impressive assortment of cured meats, dried and fresh fruit.

When we get there, Leo is waiting for us. He's literally reserved us a table, which really isn't necessary, but he does it anyway; and he's ordered a plate of just about everything for us.

My mom even convinced John to come along with us this time. He was hesitant at first, but eventually gave in. He is slowly and steadily becoming a permanent fixture of our family, I think. To be honest, I'm still not exactly sure how I feel about him and his place here; however, being uncertain is better than knowing that I absolutely don't want him here. What I mean to say is, we've made some strides.

"Order whatever you want," Leo insists, passing out menus.

Mom accepts a menu from Leo and says, "I think you already have. Good grief, Leo. We can't eat this much."

Leo holds up his hand to stop her. "We've got some new meads ready. Grendel has been a popular choice." He points to a description of the mead on the menu.

"Grendel?" Hayden says. "Lemme guess. Dad named that one, right?"

Leo winks at Hayden. "You got it, kiddo." Grendel is the monster in *Beowulf*, my dad's favorite epic poem behind *The Odyssey*. (And, remember, it was *Beowulf* that gave him the idea about the meadery in the first place. That, and an innocent comment made by a student in his class.)

But Hayden, who also shared an affinity for the old Anglo-Saxon tale, asks, "Why the heck wouldn't he name it after the hero? He named it after the monster who gets his arm chopped off."

"Because," Mom says, still reading over the selections,

"Grendel has a more assertive sound to it. It also sounds like the name of a beer, so it'll attract a different crowd."

Leo smiles. "Exactly. So, you want to try it?" When Mom nods her head, he looks at John, "And what about you, John? Care to partake?"

John's hand rubs at his stomach. "Better not. Stomach's feeling a bit temperamental today. I'll just stick with water."

Surprisingly, we devour most of the snacks, so much so that Leo actually brings us a second plate of cheese and fruit. He also brings a second and then a third round of mead for Mom. The glasses aren't too big, but I can tell that she's feeling pretty good because she's wearing a stupid, silly grin on her face, sort of like the one I had when I drank a little too much mead myself.

Then, as if out of nowhere, Sarah is standing beside our table. "Hi!" she says. She's wearing a black apron around her waist and a yellow T-shirt with the meadery's logo.

"You work here?" I ask, unable to hide my surprise.

"Yeah," she says, taking some empty plates from our table. "Just bussing tables and doing some dishes. I'm not allowed to serve — well, not the mead — because I'm not eighteen."

John hands her his plate. "Thank you," he says. That's when I notice that his plate is too clean, nothing like the messes on our plates. I quickly try to remember if I saw him eat anything.

"You're welcome," Sarah says. "Do you want me to clear away anything else for you?"

Mom grins up at her. "Nope. We're good." When

Sarah disappears into the back of the meadery, Mom leans over and whispers, "Is she still seeing Victor?"

I jerk my head back. "Why're you asking? How do you even *know* to ask that?"

"I *am* friends with her mother, remember? Besides, how else am I going to keep up with all the news regarding you and your friends? You never tell me anything about them anymore."

"I thought you didn't like gossip."

"I don't. But it's not gossiping when it's about my boys."

"And what's Sarah's relationship with Victor got to do with me?"

Mom picks up what's left of her mead and sends me a knowing look over the rim of her glass. She used to joke that she had this thing called Mom Vision, which meant that she could see and know everything about us, even the stuff we didn't want her to know (*especially* that stuff). I'm wondering suddenly, like I did when I was so much younger, if this Mom Vision might actually be a real thing. Either that, or I am just way too transparent. I mean, first Murphy; now, my mom. I really need to work on my poker face.

I'm trying to think of some smartass remark to say to my mother, one that might make her doubt her maternal instincts, when suddenly John clutches at his stomach and nearly falls out of his chair.

"*John!*" Hayden and Mom yell. Mom is trying to help him regain his balance, and Hayden jumps up to hold his chair steady. I just keep the table from tipping over.

"I'm okay," he insists.

"We should take you to the hospital, John," Mom says. "Just to be safe."

John waves her away. "No, no. I told you, my stomach's just bothering me today."

Hayden, who's still by his side, says, "It bothers you every day. That's why you take all those pills. Admit it."

John makes an effort to laugh, but it's difficult. "Those pills are just vitamins, Hayden. I'm just having a bad case of heartburn right now, is all. Nothing that a handful of Tums won't fix." He reaches into his pocket and pulls out some money. "Parker," he says, "would you run down to the pharmacy and pick up some antacids?"

"Put your money away, John," Mom says, helping him out of his chair.

"Yeah," I say, "I'll be right back."

"Parker," Mom calls after me, "just meet us back at the house. I'm going to get John home. Leo can drive us."

"Okay," I say, and start to head out the door.

I'm only about a half a block from The Beehive when I hear footsteps behind me. I turn around and see Sarah chasing me down the sidewalk. "Is he okay? Your grandfather, I mean?"

"I don't know. He says he is. It's just heartburn, I guess." I'm walking fast, which means Sarah's nearly running just to keep up with my long strides.

"That didn't look like 'just heartburn' to me."

"I didn't know you were a doctor?" My tone is a lot harsher than I had intended, but I can't help it. I'm actually a little worried about John. (And I'm embarrassed by my mom's all-too-accurate observations.)

"Parker." Sarah stops walking, which forces me to stop, too. We're standing in front of The Scoop, and the line is massive as usual. To avoid being overheard, Sarah moves closer to me and whispers, "I'm just worried about you. It's a lot to handle. First your dad; now him. I don't want anything else *bad* to happen to you. You don't deserve it. You're too...*good*."

I don't know what to say because I am totally, one hundred percent confused. From Sarah, I don't know if being good is a compliment or a criticism. Based on her soft tone and toe-shuffling stance, I'd guess that she's giving me a compliment, but guesses generally don't do anyone any good. Still, I say, "Thanks," and then turn to resume my mission.

"Parker," she says, running after me again. This time, she grabs my arm. "Seriously. If you ever need to just talk, I'm here. Really."

A warm breeze lifts Sarah's hair and I'm hit with the scent of her shampoo again, like I was when we were at the party. Vanilla, apple, the sweet musk of a forest. It's intoxicating. It almost makes me forget what I'm supposed to be doing. Then, as if by magic, her lips are touching mine. It's a brief kiss. By some standards, it could barely be considered one, especially since I didn't even have time to respond. Her lips were on mine, and then they weren't. It's quite possible that I merely imagined the whole thing.

But I know I didn't because I can still taste her lip gloss after she's gone.

Somehow, I manage to buy John's Tums and find my

way home, but it's not easy because everything seems a little hazy, like in a watercolor painting, when nothing is ever quite clear.

CHAPTER 24

Haunted by Waters

This morning I catch John standing by the door to the attic. It's open, like it always is.

Before I realize what I'm doing, I say, "Do you want to go up there?"

John turns to face me. "Would that be all right?"

"Yeah," I assure him. "If Dad were here, he'd want to show you."

I follow John up the stairs, which creak and moan under our weight. When we reach the attic, he sort of spins around slowly, as if taking in a panoramic view of a strange and lovely vista. "I don't think I've ever seen this many books. Not considering a library, of course," observes John, who looks a bit overwhelmed.

"I know. Impressive, isn't it?"

"Sure is."

It's somehow easier than I thought it would be, standing in this space with John. It's hotter than hell, though, so I open a window and turn on the box fan that's sitting on top of a bookshelf, taking up precious real estate.

"The best way to get to know Dad," I say, "is through his books." At least, that was his philosophy. Whenever he went to someone's house for the first time, he'd always search for their book collection. And it had to be a collection in order for him to be satisfied. To his credit, though, he never judged *what* they collected. Fiction or nonfiction, romance or mystery, literary or pulp. It didn't matter. It only mattered that the person read. "Never trust a person who says he hates to read, Parker. Never," he'd warn, wagging his finger at me.

John is standing in a shifting wedge of light. Whenever the light lands on his face, his wrinkles appear more defined, deep as the cracks in a dry riverbed. He also looks undeniably sad. Finally, he mumbles, "Thank you, Parker."

"For what?"

"For letting me come up here."

"Oh, well, you're welcome."

I want to check the wooden toolbox, see if Hayden returned Dad's journals, but I don't want to draw attention to them. I'm not ready to offer them up to John. Not yet. The books will have to be enough for now.

He spots a book on my dad's desk. He looks at me and then gestures toward the book, as if he's asking permission to pick it up.

I nod. "Go ahead."

John picks up the book and holds it as if it were a precious relic, a fine jewel. He turns it over in his hands and touches the pages with care. From where I'm standing, I can't read the title, but I can see that the book has seen better days. The cover is tattered; the spine loose. The pages, too, seem as if they're about to fall away, ready to catch a current of wind and drift happily to nowhere.

"What is it?" I ask.

He smiles. "*A River Runs through It*," he answers. "Have you read it?"

"Yeah. But I didn't really like it. Dad said it was just because I'm too young to appreciate it. He said that there are certain books that need to be read at a certain age. Like *Catcher in the Rye*. He always said that it's a novel that must be read by the age of twenty-five, otherwise you'll hate it."

"He had a good point there."

"Yeah."

"Did he like this book? *A River Runs through It*?"

"He said he liked the poetry of it. He always cared more about the language of a story, and not so much about the plot."

"How the story is told," John says, mostly to himself.

"Yeah."

John opens the book and reads, just to himself at first, but then he starts reading the words aloud. His voice, though soft and fragile, fills the space. "Eventually, all things merge into one, and a river runs through it." He stops, runs his hand across the bottom of the page, as if the letters are raised like braille, then whispers, "I am haunted by waters." He closes the book and seems to study the cover for a moment before he says,

"You know, I've read this book over a dozen times, and I still never tire of it."

"Take it," I say, which surprises John. Hell, it even surprises me. But it feels right, letting him have it.

"Really?"

"Yeah. Really. And take as much time as you want up here."

"Your mom won't mind?"

I shake my head, run a hand through my hair, suddenly feeling embarrassed by my generosity. "Well, considering the fact that she wanted you to stay here, I'd say no. Plus, if she wanted his office to be off limits, she would've shut the door. She has no problem setting boundaries when she wants to. Believe me."

John smiles, obviously feeling reassured. "All right then. Thank you, Parker."

In the hallway outside my room, there's a photograph of Dad hanging on the wall. He's in his kayak, waving at whoever is standing on the shore taking the picture. The water looks calm and smooth as glass, and the shore is littered with stones. Behind him is a cliff with pine trees clinging to it, their roots holding on tight, like clenched fists.

Yes, I think. *We are all haunted by waters.*

CHAPTER 25

Missing Our Dads

"Dude," Noah complains, holding up his hands, "look at my hands. It looks like I molested Strawberry Shortcake." His hands are completely red, dyed from having picked strawberries every morning for weeks. "It won't come out."

"I know. I'm tired of looking like I murdered somebody," Dante says. His hands are just as bad.

"At least you don't smell like a latte every damn day," I add, trying to commiserate.

"Please," Tony says, dismissing me.

"Yeah," Noah says, "you smell like The Mill. People's eyes practically roll to the back of their heads when they walk into that place, it smells so good. It's probably, like, the best cologne in the world."

"Sure," I say, wiping some sweat from my forehead with

the back of my hand, "it really drives the women wild. I have to fight 'em off with a stick."

It's too hot to sit in the shed, so we're in Gabe and Tony's yard, sitting around an inflatable kiddie pool with our feet in the water and our shirts off. Tony is the designated Snack Man, which basically means he is manning the cooler and rationing the solitary bag of pretzel nuggets. Whenever we want a pretzel, we say, "Nug me," and Tony tosses us a few. Actually, it would be more accurate to say that he pelts us with them.

"Anybody want a drink?" Tony asks.

"What's in the cooler? Anything good?" Dante wants to know.

Tony opens it and moves some ice around. "Just soda. Diet mostly."

"No, thanks," Dante says, a pretzel nugget hanging from his bottom lip. "Too many preservatives. You might as well drink embalming fluid."

Noah chuckles. "I guess we better take your word on that one."

"Yep," Dante says. "You should."

"Eh. Who cares? Toss me one," I say, desperate for something cold to drink.

For the rest of the afternoon, we chase the shade around Gabe and Tony's yard, moving the kiddie pool and our foldable lawn chairs every hour or so. To be honest, it's the most relaxed I've felt in a long time. I even consider telling them about Sarah, that she kissed me, but I don't know how they'd take it. They think Victor is an asshole sometimes, yes; but he's *our* asshole, which still requires a certain level of loyalty.

"No way," Noah says, reading a text.

"What?" I ask.

"Victor's dad. He got arrested."

"For *what*?" Dante says, shifting to the edge of his chair.

Noah scrolls through the message. "I guess he was pulled over for speeding, but then they found a bunch of pills in his car."

"Wow," Dante says half-heartedly, mostly because it's not really all that shocking.

"Was it Victor who texted you?" I ask.

Noah nods. "Yeah."

Tony stands up and stretches. "That really sucks."

Gabe, quiet as usual, just nods in agreement.

The entire yard is shaded now, and it feels much cooler, as if a storm might be brewing in the distance. In the neighbor's yard, there are five boys, maybe seven or eight years old, playing hide and seek. They could be us, forever ago. Without even realizing it, we're all watching them as they try to find places to hide; some of them settling for places in plain sight, others choosing to squeeze into dark, tight spaces, like under the deck.

The neighbor, Mr. Franklin, steps out on the deck with a plate of hot dogs. When he sees us, he gives us a quick wave with a pair of tongs. "Gentlemen," he calls, but he's not talking to us; he's talking to his son and his son's friends. When they see him, they come running like a wild herd.

"Dinner ready yet?" Mr. Franklin's son asks.

"Nope. About to get it going, though. I'll let you boys

know when it's ready," replies Mr. Franklin.

Watching them, I suspect that most of us are feeling the same thing, which is that we are missing our dads. When someone you love dies, the missing never goes away. It's always there, but sometimes it's more settled, like silt in a river. Then there are times, like now, when something churns it up, and the missing rises closer to the surface.

Then Dante says, "Victor must really hate his dad."

"No," Gabe says, "He loves him. He just wants his dad to love him back."

CHAPTER 26

The Unexpected Truth

John asked me to go fishing again; and since we've been getting along, I've relented and agreed to go with him. So yesterday, I pulled the tarp from the canoe and checked the yoke and thwarts, just to make sure they weren't loose; and I dug out the tackle box and fishing rods from the bowels of the garage. Since neither one of us has fished in a while, we've decided it would be best to just use live bait. Trying to figure out how to tie the old flies is a challenge that neither one of us really wants.

But last night, when John suggested that we fish the Glendale River, my stomach cinched up again. See, the mouth of the Glendale River empties into Haywood Lake at Talisa Bay, and when most people canoe "down the Glen," they end up following it straight to the bay. Just the thought of being anywhere near that river or in that bay or on that lake makes me sick because, after all, it's the water that took my father.

I could blame his heart, but it doesn't seem right to blame something so good.

Still, I could see in John's face that he really wanted to go there. "Maybe he needs closure," Mom suggested, but I could see in her face that even she was unnerved by the thought of my going there and being too close to where it happened. "Parker, you don't have to go if you don't want to," she told me last night before she went to bed.

"Mom, I thought you'd be happy about this. I mean, isn't this what you wanted? For us to *bond*?"

"Yes, but it's understandable if you don't want to go *there*. You could go to Ridge Creek or the pond over at the park or even that manmade lake in the housing development near Glendale. They allow anyone to fish there. I mean, I honestly don't even know what he's *thinking*, wanting to take you there." It was the first time I'd heard her be critical of John in any way. Until that point, she'd been giving him the benefit of the doubt for just about everything.

Apparently, it was my turn to come to his defense. "It'll be okay. We'll just...stay on the river," I said, trying to convince both of us.

"You're sure?" She was wearing the blue robe again, the one she wore for weeks after Dad died. I hoped it wasn't a bad sign.

"Yes," I lied.

We wake up before dawn, which isn't difficult for me because I'm always up this early. I don't even really need an alarm clock anymore, my body's so used to it. John is an early riser, too, so he's already waiting for me in the kitchen. I open the fridge to make us some sandwiches to bring, but apparently Mom beat me to it, so I just toss them in the cooler along with some bottles of water and a random selection of fruit from the bowl on the counter. Apples, oranges, a couple of plums.

We tied the canoe to the top of John's truck after dinner last night and went out and got some bait, so the only thing left to do is drive to the river. It's only a half hour drive or so, but longer this morning since John is driving. Neither one of us says much, choosing instead to focus on the headlights pushing through the stubborn fog.

John turns down a gravel road that leads to one of the boat launches along the river. We park as close as we can to the shoreline so that we don't have to carry the canoe too far. After we've loaded the tackle and rods and cooler, I hand John the oars and push us off before hopping into the canoe and taking my seat at the stern.

We paddle in silence, but we don't have to work too hard because the current is strong and steady. Small waves splash against the sides of the canoe with a satisfying thwack. The sun is peeking past a hill of clouds, its light catching on the surface of the water, making it look like ripples of gold. Then my memory starts to get the best of me. Suddenly, I am remembering the last time I was on this river. It was with my dad and Hayden, last summer, on a morning very similar to this one. We were meandering down the river, letting the current push us along, our oars barely touching the surface of the water. Dad was at the stern, where I am now. He was telling us to look at the water, to see how it glowed and shimmered in the sun. "What would you say it looks like, Hayden?" he'd asked. He was always testing our ability to come up with an unusual simile or metaphor, something original that still rang true.

"I'd say," Hayden said, pausing to think, "I'd say it looks like wrinkled silk, like one of those robes that Indian ladies wear."

My dad stifled a laugh and said, "Creative. And what about you, Parker?"

I remember that I thought quite a while about it. I wanted to impress him. Finally, after several minutes, I just gave up and said, "It looks like peace." My dad was quiet, which I assumed meant that he was disappointed, but then he said, "I agree."

Anyway, a few miles downriver, we find a spot where the fishing seems promising. Some boulders line the edge of the river and even jut up from its middle, like lost whales coming up for air. Just beyond the boulders are some eddies, places where the current slows and circles back on itself. We pull the canoe to shore, clumsily bait our hooks, and cast our lines, nearly entangling them mid-cast.

"Sorry," Johns says, reeling in his line a bit. "Guess I'm rustier than I thought."

"Me, too."

But it's not just lack of practice; it's nerves, too. My entire body is shaking, and sweat is beginning to drip down my temples and my back. I know that my dad didn't die here, but this is close enough. It's enough to make me think that I see the underside of his kayak in one of the eddies, spinning like the hands of a clock, counting the seconds he's underwater. I close my eyes, hard, trying to will the image away. And I'm wishing, more than anything, that I had taken my mom's advice.

Then I feel a sharp tug at the end of my line.

"You got one!" shouts John.

The rod is bending in agony. I pull back hard, stumbling backward. The line is taut, and I'm struggling to reel it in. I decide to let the reel go a bit, feeling it spin beneath my hand, and then try again. Slowly, the line shortens, and whatever it is at the end of it starts to give up its fight.

"Keep reeling! You got it!" John shouts again as he moves toward me. He's already taken his line out of the river.

Finally, I grab the line with my hand and pull the fish from the water. It's swinging wildly, bending its whole body back and forth, as if it could swim through the air. I somehow manage to hook my finger in his lip and then set him down on a platform of granite, waiting for him to give up his fight. But he doesn't.

John's next to me now. "Rainbow trout. I'd say at least two feet long. Doesn't look too happy, does he?"

"No."

"Well done, though. He's a beauty. Definitely something worth bragging about."

"Thanks. But it doesn't take much effort to put a worm on a hook." I'm feeling bad because the hook is caught in the trout's cheek and it's tearing his flesh. He's still struggling, but his flopping has slowed to a quiet twitch.

"You can toss him back in if you want." John picks up the fish and maneuvers the hook from his cheek with a single, deft move.

"Yeah," I say, watching his mouth open and close, "let him go." John holds the trout until it's completely submerged, and then he lets go of it, gently. It swims away from us, disappearing under some frothy waves.

"Hungry?" John asks.

"Starving."

It's not even eight o'clock yet, but we didn't have breakfast, so we unpack our sandwiches and fruit and sit on the rocks to eat. The occasional wave splashes against the sides of the rocks, but we are mostly serenaded by the rhythm of the current. The sun is warm and feels good on my face. I even close my eyes and lounge against the back of another rock. It's weird. A few minutes ago, I wanted to be anywhere else but here, and now I feel a sense of peace pulsing through me, as if I've just been given a heavy dose of something. Maybe it's the sound of the water or the warmth of the morning sun. Maybe it's even John.

"Parker?" John says.

My eyes are still closed. I don't want to break this spell. "Yeah?"

"I need to tell you something."

"Okay."

There's a long pause and everything seems to quiet to a hush.

"Parker," he says, "I'm dying."

Dad? I think. Again, I see his kayak, spinning helplessly.

His body submerged, not even trying to fight for breath, as if it's forgotten how. My insides are tightening and twisting, a feeling that's becoming way too familiar. I open my eyes and leap to my feet. I am ready to jump in. I am ready to save him.

But he isn't here, of course.

And I realize that it wasn't my father who'd said it. It was John.

He stands, picks up his rod, and casts. With his back to me, he says, "I've been wanting to tell you, since I got here, but I didn't know how. I had planned on telling your mother right away, but I was so happy that she'd offered to have me stay with all of you that I didn't want to risk messing up the opportunity to get to know you. I kept telling myself that I needed to say something, but I just couldn't bring myself to do it."

I move to the edge of the rock, willing him to look at me, but he won't. He's just staring at the water.

"What do you mean *you're dying*?" I ask, because I can't think of another question.

"I'm sick, Parker."

"Sick?"

"Cancer." He reels in his line. Casts again.

"Cancer?" I can't help it. I keep turning his statements into questions, as if doing so might somehow make them less true. "What kind?" I ask, my voice cracking.

"It doesn't matter much anymore. Seems like it's just about everywhere now," he says, pretending to concentrate on his fishing. He won't risk looking at me.

Images from the past month flash through my mind. I see him doubled over, grabbing at his stomach. I see my mom and Hayden rush to his side. "The vitamins. They're not even vitamins, are they? They're medicine," I say, but there's not a single note of sympathy in my voice.

"Just for pain at this point. But, to tell you the truth, they're not really helping too much anymore."

I stare at the water. The current seems faster now. The eddies look like boiling cauldrons, ready to bubble over. Which is how I feel. I feel angry and hurt and, beyond anything else, betrayed. All of these emotions are coursing through me, their currents fast and furious, until they meet, whirling and roiling and threatening to pull me under.

I yank the rod from John's hand and throw it in the river. It floats away like a helpless piece of driftwood. "You tricked us," I say through gritted teeth. In fact, every part of me feels tight. My legs, my shoulders, my fists.

"Parker, no. I got your dad's letter right after I relapsed. I wanted to see him...before...I died. To make things right. I didn't know he had...until I got to Haywood. Please. That's the truth."

"No. That's *bull*shit!"

"It's not. When I checked into that motel in town, there were some old newspapers lying around. I picked one up and read about it there. I found out my son had died by reading it in the paper. It was...I can't even describe it. I had finally worked up the courage to face him, and he was gone. I was going to turn around and head home, but before I knew it, I was asking the lady at the desk about it and about where I might find Grace, and she sent me to The Mill. That's when I first saw you, remember? And then I left the note at your house. I hadn't planned on staying, but your mom insisted. And then I just wanted to get to know you all. I should've told you, I know that, but it seemed better not to. It wasn't a trick."

"You don't get to call him that," I say, seething.

"What?"

"Your son. You don't get to call him that. You walked out and didn't come back until he was dead."

"Parker, I — "

"No. I mean, you must know how messed up this is, right? What did you expect? Are we just supposed to take *care* of you now? It's not our fault that you're all alone and don't have anybody else. That's your *own* fault. That's the life you chose for yourself. You can't just use us to fill in the blanks."

"That's not what I want, Parker. I never expected anything from you. I only wanted — "

"Stop!" I say, taking a step backward, wanting nothing more than to get away from him. "Just stop. I don't really give a shit what you want. God, I can't even believe my dad ever wanted to find you." I pause. A thought enters my head, like a rodent that squeezed its way through the tiniest of holes. It's the kind of thought that I'd trap and just toss out, too dirty and plagued to actually say out loud. But I decide to say it and risk sounding nothing like my father's son. "I'm glad he died before you got here. You don't deserve him."

CHAPTER 27

Et tu, Charlie?

Before John can respond, I am bounding up one of the hills that flanks the river, climbing my way to the nearest road. My mom is supposed to pick us up downriver around noon and then drive us and the canoe back to John's truck, but there's no way that I'm about to spend another minute with him. And I really can't face my mom, either. No doubt she'll be angry with me for speaking to the old man the way I did *and* for leaving him there. But I don't care. When she finds out the truth, she'll understand. At least, I think so. I used to be able to predict her moves with a fair amount of accuracy. Now, I just don't know anymore.

I feel like I don't know *anything* anymore.

The last part of the hill is quite steep, so I have to crawl up, grabbing at roots and rocks for some leverage. It feels like everything is breaking loose beneath me, like I'm not even on solid ground. It's just dust and ash and dead, brittle leaves. When I finally reach the top, I brush myself off and try to get my bearings straight, looking up and down the road. I recognize the country store to my left and figure out that I'm on Hamlin Road, which means that if I start heading south, I'll make my way back to Haywood. If I head north, I'd be on my way to Glendale, where Murphy lives.

I have to admit, I do take one or two steps in her direction, but then I think better of it, and start to head home.

I just walk along for a while, kicking at stones, trying to calm my nerves. The roadside is littered with crushed beer cans, paper cups, and an assortment of roadkill, mostly flattened frogs and the occasional rag of a squirrel.

My anger is still pulsing through me, so much so that I feel like I've been electrocuted. You know, like when you get shocked plugging something into a faulty outlet. It's that kind of sharp, relentless sting that starts in the fingers and moves through your entire body.

The road is shaded, mostly by pines, which is good because the heat is penetrating now. Every once in a while, there's a clearing, some farmer's field where the sun has no obstructions and beats down on me without remorse, making it harder to breathe. It's so hot that I can even see the heat hovering above the pavement, like an aura. Once I'm in another stretch of shade, I decide to call Charlie.

" 'lo?" Charlie says.

"Charlie, it's Parker."

"I know, dude. What's up?"

I stop walking. "I need you to pick me up. Can you?"

"Sure. Where are you?"

"Hamlin Road, a little before that country store. Heading toward Haywood."

There's a pause. "What the hell are you doing out there?"

"Charlie, just pick me up. Please."

"Okay. Be there in a few."

About fifteen minutes later, I see Charlie's car heading toward me. It's easy to spot. A Mini Cooper, red with white racing stripes running up and down its hood. Convertible, too. He inherited it from his mom when she got a new car. "Hey," he says as he pulls over. He's wearing aviator sunglasses, a Polo shirt, and a pair of plaid shorts. Not his usual attire.

"Were you golfing?" I ask, sliding into the passenger seat.

"Yeah," he says as he turns the car around.

"Sorry."

"No worries, man. My dad was kicking my ass, anyway. I was happy to get outta there." He drives a mile or so and then asks, "So...ya gonna tell me what's going on? You weren't doing the walk of shame, were you? Because that's an awful far walk from Murphy's house."

"Shut up." But I smile, in spite of myself. I'm actually grateful for the harassment right now. It tempers my anger, dropping it to a moderate simmer.

"Seriously, though," he says, losing his teasing grin, "what's going on?"

So, I tell him. In one long, rambling sentence. I don't even think I stop to breathe.

Charlie listens without saying anything. He doesn't even offer a sympathetic nod. He just drives, his eyes focused on the road. But when we reach Main Street, he turns right and parks near the meadery. "What're we doing here?" I ask, not really caring. If he had dropped me off at home, I would have told him to take me somewhere else. So, it might as well be The Beehive.

"You look like I need a drink," he says, slapping me on the knee and relishing one of his favorite lines.

"Is it even open right now?"

He holds up his keys. "It's always open when you have a key."

Inside, Charlie makes his way behind the counter and grabs two glasses, one noticeably smaller than the other. "What'll it be? Grendel? Bee Spit? Spring Fling?"

"What's with these names?"

"Hey. Blame your dad."

"I wish I could."

Charlie reaches over the counter and squeezes my shoulder. "Grendel it is then." He fills the smaller glass and slides it over to me before helping himself to some mead. "So," he says, "John."

"Yeah?"

"He told you he's dying and you just left him there? At the river?"

"No. He has the canoe. He'll be fine."

Charlie crosses his arms, leans against the counter. "That's not really what I mean."

"So what do you mean then?"

He looks down at his feet and shakes his head. "Parker, you know I love you like a brother, so I feel like I can say this to you."

"Say what?" I ask, gulping down the rest of my mead.

"You're being a dick."

I look at him. Confused. Hurt. I thought he'd be on my side. I thought he'd understand. "No," I say, which is officially the worst defense in the world.

"No?" he snorts. "Your grandfather tells you he's dying and your reaction is to just run away and then call me to come and rescue you?"

I hang my head. Being reprimanded by Charlie is unexpected, to say the least. It's worse somehow than being reprimanded by my mom. With her, I know it's just part of her job description. But it's certainly not part of Charlie's. I mean, he's supposed to be a member of *my* army, a footman in *my* battle. "He's not my grandfather," I mumble, sounding pathetic, even to myself.

"You know what?" he says, filling his glass again. "I'm sick of this 'He's not my grandfather' bullshit. The bottom line is that your dad *wanted* the guy in his life. In your life. Embrace it, man. So you feel like he tricked you. So what? Show the guy some goddamn sympathy. His son died before he got to see him again, and now *he's* dying. But he still has you and Hayden and your mom, and you're telling me that you can't give him that? Not even for the time he's got left?" He gulps down his mead and points the glass at me. "That's bullshit, Park, and you know it."

Something in me is about to break. I can feel it starting

to crack. I can feel everything, everyone, pushing against me. Squeezing me. Crushing me. "Fuck you, Charlie," I say.

And then I just walk out the door.

CHAPTER 28

When They Answer Back

I head down the alley toward Grant Street, which is just south of Main Street. There's not much on this side of town, just the library, an old toy museum that hardly anybody visits, and some dilapidated houses. You know the ones: saplings growing from their gutters, clumps of moss holding loose shingles in place, paint peeling and curling so badly it looks more like the scales of a diseased fish.

    I don't even know why I'm walking this way, especially since my house is in the opposite direction; but, quite frankly, I don't know what the hell I'm doing. I'm angry and hurt and confused and upset and sad. Mostly, though, I'm just feeling really ashamed of myself. It seems as if walking out on people has become my modus operandi, like my default mechanism has been set to escape, to run, to abandon. For a second, I wonder if it might just be in my DNA. After all, John chose to run away, so why shouldn't it make sense that I might do the same thing?

But even I know that's bullshit. Nothing more than a lame-ass excuse that fails to make me feel any better about myself. If anything, it makes me feel worse.

When I've walked a couple of blocks down Grant Street, I spot Victor and his dad who must've somehow managed to keep himself out of jail after his latest bust. They are leaving Kelly's Pub, a dive bar in town that never seems to close. Its neon sign shouts OPEN; however, the flickering red and yellow lights send the opposite message. To be honest, I've been to Kelly's a few times, but just on St. Patrick's Day for some Reubens, when every pub, no matter how rundown, is packed. It's got a huge horseshoe-shaped bar, a couple of pool tables, and graffiti all over its walls. Everyone writes on the walls at Kelly's, which I'm certain was a favorite feature of my father's. He told me once that the tradition started years ago, and rather than fighting it, the owner decided that that would be "his thing." So, he puts out pints full of Sharpies and encourages his customers to have at it. I suppose it's better than painting the place every few years.

Anyway, I'm not surprised to see Victor and his dad stumbling out of the bar. Because, you know, it would be the kind of place to serve a minor. But then I notice that Victor isn't stumbling or careening wildly, like he does when he's had too many. His dad's arm is slung over his shoulders, and he's got his hand wrapped firmly around his dad's wrist, doing his best to drag him along. I'm standing on the other side of the street, watching, hidden by a swaying curtain of willow branches. I watch Victor ease his father into the backseat of his car. He even buckles him in, as if he were a child. Victor scoots around the back of the car, steals a quick glance — I'm assuming to make sure no one's seen him — and then drives off.

Gabe's words come back to me: *He just wants his dad to love him back.*

And I have to admit, there's something about what I just witnessed that reignites my emotions, sending hot, wild flames lapping at my heart.

And then I just start running.

Before I know it, I am heading toward Haywood Cemetery. I hadn't planned on going there, of course, but my internal GPS determined this route. My heart is pounding, thumping against the inside of my ribs, pulsating like one of those blue dots that shows you where you are on the map.

There are a few people at the cemetery, an elderly woman planting flowers, a middle-aged man who's sitting in a lawn chair and reading the paper, and a family clad in black and fresh with grief. I meander quietly in and around the headstones, sort of tip-toeing among the dead, afraid I might disturb them. My dad's grave is near the top of one of the only hills in the cemetery, an expensive plot, prime real estate for the dead. My mom chose it "for the view." I remember thinking that she sounded a little crazy when she'd said that. I mean, she's never been one to think that the dead can come back and mingle among us, undetected. But then I realized that she didn't choose the plot for Dad. She chose it for us.

Come to think of it, when someone you love dies, many of the choices you have to make aren't really about the person who has died. You tell yourself that they are, but they aren't. They are about you and what you need to help you deal with the fact that your person is gone. Yes, you're honoring him, but mostly what you're doing is remembering. I don't think there's anything wrong with this. I just think it's the truth. You do what you do in order to survive all of the *surviving*.

When I reach my dad's grave, I'm out of breath and panting like a dog. I'm so tired that I have to lean over and grip the tops of my knees for support. Finally, when my heart slows its frantic rhythm, I just stand there and stare at my father's headstone.

Then, after what seems like forever, I close my eyes and feel words forming in my mouth. But they catch, like burs. I want to talk to him. Really, I do. It's weird, though, talking to a slab of granite.

"Just go ahead," I hear someone say behind me. It's the newspaper man, the guy who was sitting in the lawn chair just a few minutes ago.

"What?"

"You want to talk to the person? Just go ahead. It's a little strange at first — sorta makes you feel like a crazy person, don't it? — but then it feels right. Sometimes, if you really listen, they even answer back."

Newspaper man is a crazy person, I think. Still, I nod and tell him "Thank you" and then he moves along, his paper tucked under one arm and his chair hooked on the other.

I clear my throat. Look around. "Dad," I whisper.

"Dad?" I say again, bending a little so that my ear is next to his headstone, stupidly trying to listen.

I sit down and rest my head on his name. I won't lie. There's part of me that wants to wrap my arms around it. "Dad," I say, my forehead pressing against the J of his name. "Tell me what to do. Please. Tell me."

Nothing. No response. Why would there be? I don't know why I even expected one. Still, I'm disappointed and feeling more lost than ever.

Until I lean back and see the date. That's when I remember what I had forgotten, what had been the one thing that convinced me to give John a chance to begin with.

I've been carrying my father's letter to John around with me since my mom gave it to me. I guess as a reminder, should I need one. I take it out of my wallet and look at the date on the envelope and then again on the stone. They're still the same. I touch the date on my father's grave, slide my fingers across it.

Maybe the newspaper man was right.

Sometimes, they even answer back.

CHAPTER 29

Facing Mom

A few hours later, I'm walking up our narrow driveway, slowly. My mom's car and John's truck are both there, and the canoe is leaning upside-down against the garage, as if frowning at me, unable to hide its disappointment. My hand is shaking as I open the gate to the backyard. I'm actually hoping I can sneak in, but the gate gives a baleful moan, betraying me, letting me know that there will be no getting away with anything. Not that I think I should.

My mom is sitting on the patio, waiting for me. I expect to see her face pinched tight with accusation, but when she sees me, she just stands up and hugs me. "John told me. He told me everything."

"I'm sorry," I mumble into her shoulder. "I was a jerk."

Mom pulls away from me, reaches up, cups my face in

her hands. Her eyes are moving back and forth, like she's trying to read my thoughts. "I don't blame you for being upset, but — "

"I know," I interrupt. "I shouldn't have left him there."

"No, you shouldn't have. But it had to have been hard. Being at the water, thinking about your dad, finding out about John. Hell, here you are — here *we* are — just getting to know him and…." her voice trails off, her words catching on the wind like a dandelion seed. Then she says, "He's not upset with you, you know. He understands."

We're sitting now, side by side, on the steps that lead to the backdoor. "Where is he?" I ask. "I owe him an apology, at least."

"Inside. With Hayden."

My face flushes with shame. I hadn't even thought about Hayden. "Does Hay know?"

Mom takes a deep breath. "Yes. John told both of us. Together." Mom stops, rubs at her temples, and then clasps her hands together. "Is it awful that I'm actually relieved that I didn't have to tell Hayden myself? It's bad enough knowing, but having to tell someone else? It was a burden I was relieved not to have had."

We both stare straight ahead then, and I know why. We are both thinking about that Wednesday night, when she had to tell us about Dad. I'm not sure that weight has ever lifted from her, and I'm not sure it ever will.

"How did Hayden handle the news?" I say, breaking this dangerous trance we're both in.

Mom smiles. "You know Hay. He just got up and

hugged John and said, 'Don't worry. We'll take care of you,' as if there was no other option."

"He's a better man than I am, I guess." The shame on my face is now spreading to my neck and chest, growing like a poisonous vine, threatening to strangle me.

"Don't be too hard on yourself." But there's some part of her that knows I'm right, that Hayden is just better in some ways than I am. He's more open, more forgiving, more willing to embrace what he doesn't really understand. I actually shared this observation with Mom a while back, sometime before Dad died. Her response was simple: "You're the oldest." That's all she said, as if that was enough of an explanation.

"So what're we going to do?" I ask.

"About John? I don't know. Take his lead, I guess. But I've already told him that he can stay with us. I hope that's okay with you."

"Are you really asking if it's okay?" I say, recalling how she didn't care much about my opinion before, when she'd invited him to stay with us in the first place.

"Yes. I am."

"Well, we can't exactly kick him out now, can we?"

"We can make other arrangements."

Laughter suddenly erupts from inside of the house and finds its way out the window and into the hot afternoon air. It's John and Hayden. "No," I say, "I think our arrangements are fine the way they are."

"Good," Mom says.

CHAPTER 30

Dating Advice

Mom is on a mission. Now that we know the truth about John, she is calling doctors, making appointments, doing research, filling prescriptions, buying vitamins. *Juicing*, for God's sake. I think she thinks she can save him, which is kind of scary because I don't want her to risk getting her hopes up. Hell, I don't want her to get *John's* hopes up. At this point, I think he just likes being cared for, a feeling that must be pretty foreign to him.

I haven't spoken to Charlie since he picked me up from Hamlin Road, mostly because I've been too embarrassed to call him. I can't avoid him forever, though, especially since we're scheduled to work some overlapping shifts this week.

Today is one of those days.

Since my mom wants me around to help out with John

during the day (not that he needs much help yet), she's scheduled me for the later shifts, which is tough getting used to. It also kind of sucks because now my schedule is totally different from the guys' schedule. Afternoons of lounging around the kiddie pool in Gabe and Tony's backyard will be few and far between for me now.

When I get to the coffeehouse today, Madge is already heading out the door. She's actually wearing a dress, which I don't think I've ever seen her in before. Actually, it looks more like a woman's suit, but it's difficult to tell because she's in a hurry. Dress or suit, the effect is the same: She looks older. And prettier, something I did not think was possible. "You look nice, Madge," I say as she passes me, my voice taking on a tone that suggests that she normally doesn't look nice, which could not be further from the truth.

"Thanks," she says.

"Going someplace special?" I ask, sounding a little too much like a creeper.

"Wouldn't you like to know," she says. It's a statement, not a coy question. Still, I need something to make me feel better, so I'm going to go ahead and tell myself that we just had ourselves a flirtatious interlude. A little harmless delusion never hurt anyone, right?

Charlie is behind the counter, scooping up some coffee beans that didn't quite make it into the grinder. He flashes me a quick look, but before he can say anything, Nils barges in through the back. "How's it going, guys?" he says, carrying several white cake boxes in his arms. He is also wearing a faded T-shirt and pajama pants that are covered in a fine dusting of flour, and I'm pretty sure that he's got some sort of cream or syrup in his hair.

"Great, man," Charlie answers, "how are you?"

"Can't complain. Too much." Nils sets the boxes down and opens them, one by one.

"And what do we have here?" Charlie asks, checking out the cakes.

Nils stands back, admiring his work. "Layered coconut cake with lemon curd and vanilla bean cheesecake with a chocolate ganache and raspberry sauce. And chocolate cake. You know, for the unadventurous type." As usual, he's already pre-sliced them.

"You've upped your game, Nils," I say, noting the chocolate curls and what looks like gold foil decorating the top of the cheesecake.

Nils puffs his chest out a bit, even rubs his stomach. "Yep. I was getting bored. And I figure if I'm bored, then so is everybody else. I hope your mom doesn't mind that I took some liberties with her order."

"Doubt it," I say. "She trusts you."

"Cool." As usual, he checks out how his cakes look from the front of the counter. He bends over, squats, looks at them from a couple of different angles. When he's finally satisfied, he says, "Well, I'll be back tomorrow morning."

"You want a coffee to go?" Charlie asks.

"Nah. I'm already too hopped up on sugar. Thanks, though." Nils waves and leaves through the front of the coffeehouse. On his way out, though, he trips on the mat in front of the door and stumbles. "*Sonofabitch*!" he yells as he regains his balance and stomps out the door.

Charlie and I both laugh, and then, just because I want to get it out of the way, I say, "So...about the other day."

"Don't worry about it," he says, waving his hand at me. "I'm the one who should apologize. I overstepped and it wasn't cool and I'm sorry."

"No. You were right. I needed to hear it. I'm sorry."

There's an awkward spot of silence, as if this shared apology has somehow shifted something between us. It's not a bad shift, necessarily. Just different. Maybe we both realize how vulnerable we are, and can be, with each other. My dad would be proud, too. His motto was never to follow an apology with the word *but*. "It's not real if you offer an excuse. Or worse, if you end with an accusation. The strongest apology is the one that stands alone."

"I thought Murphy was working today," I say, pushing the silence aside.

Charlie punches me in the arm. "You mean your girlfriend?"

And we're back, I think, smiling. "She's not my girlfriend," I protest.

"You seemed pretty chummy to me the last time I saw you together."

"Can't a guy and girl just be friends?" I ask, making an iced coffee for myself.

Charlie looks toward the ceiling, as if the answer might fall from the rafters. "Uh, no," he says, "usually not. Anyway, why *not* date Murphy? She's cool. Edgy. Not some cookie-cutter chick, you know what I mean? Plus, I like that she gives you shit. You need a girl who challenges you."

"Yeah. I guess." There's no doubt that Murphy's cool and fun and smart and unlike most other girls I know, but my mind is just too preoccupied with Sarah, leaving little room for anybody else in the Love Department. And, despite everything, I haven't stopped thinking about that moment when she touched her lips against mine.

Did it mean anything? I don't know. There are too many variables that could change its meaning. Her history with Victor, Victor's being my friend, Victor's dad's arrest, John's illness, my dad's death. It's a kiss open to way too many interpretations; plus, it doesn't help that I haven't seen Sarah since it happened.

I realize that I feel a little disconnected from everyone, like the links in our chain have broken. Summer is partially to blame. But it's also something bigger, as if our lives have already begun pulling us in different directions, demanding more of us, breaking us apart.

But mostly, it's dads who are dead.

Or just deadbeat.

CHAPTER 31

What's More Interesting than Death?

John, despite my mom's valiant efforts, is noticeably weaker. Day by day, he seems like a thinner version of himself, as if his cancer won't stop whittling away at him, carving him out from the inside until he's nothing but flesh and bone.

But he doesn't seem to slow down. In fact, he still insists on taking his turn making dinner (not that he eats much of it himself) or doing dishes or fixing whatever he can, even if it's as simple as changing a lightbulb. My mom, of course, keeps telling him to rest, but he responds with "Grace, as long as I can, I want to be of use. I can't just sit around and...*wait*."

Tonight, Mom and Hayden are at the drive-in. They wanted us to go, too, but John said he was too tired and I just didn't like the movie choices. Plus, when John said that he didn't want to go, Mom basically threw me the look that said, *You should stay here.*

"You want to play cards or something?" I ask John after we've cleaned up after dinner.

John collapses into a chair. "Nah. My brain's in a bit of a fog tonight. How about we just talk?"

"Sure." I fill two glasses of water and set them on the table.

"How about something stronger?"

"Really?"

"Eh. Why not? I gave your dad his first beer when he was around fifteen, I think."

"Really?" I say again. "He never told me that."

"Wasn't a regular thing. He had just finished helping me shingle the house. It was hotter than blazes. The occasion just called for it, I guess."

I open the fridge and move some bottles of condiments around. I spot a few bottles of beer in the back. I have no idea how long they've been there, though. Months probably. I grab two bottles, twist the tops off with the bottom of my T-shirt, and set them on the table. John picks one up, suspends it in the air, and says, "Cheers, Parker."

"Cheers," I say back before I take a long swig.

John just sips his beer, cautiously, probably afraid that his stomach will revolt, as it usually does these days. He holds the bottle under the light, studies the label. "Tastes pretty good."

"Yeah. It does."

"Think your mom will be mad?"

"Only if she finds out."

"I suppose this isn't your first beer."

I consider lying to him but decide not to. "Nope. It's not."

"Don't worry," he says. "Mum's the word."

We take another drink. It's strange. I had imagined this day, but it wasn't with John. It was with my dad. I'd pictured us sitting by the lake, laughing, drinking beer, telling stories. You know, just like friends, like what a father and son would eventually become if we'd been given the time.

John starts peeling the label from the sweating bottle. "So, how's your friend Sarah?"

"Fine, I guess."

"You like her."

"Why is everyone all the sudden so interested in my love life? Or lack thereof?" I'm annoyed, but not too much, which is surprising. Maybe it's just the beer, already doing its thing, calming my nerves before they start their usual unraveling.

"Because, love is more interesting than death, don't you think?"

This catches me off guard. Sort of takes my breath away for a minute. I run my hands along the edge of the table, which has been worn smooth, like a pebble in a river. My head is spinning now, thinking about all the ways in which my world has been turned upside down since my dad died. And since John drifted into our lives. So I say, "Love is definitely *better* than death, but death is anything but dull."

"Yes. I suppose you're right about that." John leans back in his chair, away from the light. He crosses his arms on his chest, and I can't help but notice how weak they look, just loose skin draped over bone, like wet clothes on a line. Then I see a smile stretch across his face. "You know," he says, rubbing his chin, "I always had a feeling that your dad would marry Grace."

"Really? Why?" I ask, remembering what Dad had written in his letter to John. *Do you remember Grace?* he'd written. *Well, I married her. You were right back then.*

He laughs a bit, kind of to himself. "Because he used to complain about her all of the time, back when they were in elementary school. Every day it was something else Grace had done to get him in trouble. His mother and I used to joke that he and Grace were going to date each other someday. Guess we were right."

There's a long, quiet pause. I take another quick drink and say, "Did you ever think about grandma after you left?"

"Sometimes," he says. "But mostly I thought about your dad."

We're quiet again. Another question begins percolating in my head and I'm not sure if I should risk asking it, but I'm feeling like the boundaries between us are crumbling, so I go for it. "Did you ever fall in love with anyone else? I mean, after you left?"

"If you're wondering if your dad has any long-lost brothers or sisters, the answer is no."

"No. I mean, good. That's good that he doesn't. Only because I'm not sure we could handle another surprise," I say, quickly adding, "No offense."

"None taken," John says, waving his hand in front of

him.

"Did you, though? Meet someone?"

John clears his throat. "There was someone. Her name was Nancy. We never married. She died a few years back."

"Oh. I'm sorry," I say. "What was she like?"

"Oh, she was a spitfire. I met her at the diner, near where I lived. She loved — pardon the expression — busting balls. I think I fell in love with her as soon as I sat down at her counter and she gave me hell for sitting in someone else's seat."

"Did you tell her...*everything*?"

"You mean about leaving my family? Yes. She knew. She always wanted me to reach out to Jackie. Make things right. I guess she got her way, sort of."

"When did you tell her that you loved her?" I pick up my beer. It's empty now, and I really want another one because I'm enjoying this mental lubrication. Thoughts, questions, words. Everything is running more smoothly right now.

"Do you really want to know, or are you asking for your own research?"

"Are we back to my love life again?"

"You tell me."

"All right. Maybe," I say, a little embarrassed.

John leans forward, resting his elbows on the table. "When it comes to love, there's no time like the present."

"It's a little complicated when you think you might be in love with your friend's girlfriend." I flick my fingers in the air, adding air quotes around the word *girlfriend*.

"Yes. I guess that would complicate things." John pauses. His eyes seem to scan the room. Then he looks right at me and asks, "What would your dad tell you to do?"

My eyes glance up at the clock. It's getting kind of late, and I have to open the coffeehouse tomorrow. (Mom finally gave me a morning shift again.) I pick up the bottles and notice that John has barely drunk much of his beer, but I don't say anything about it. I just rinse them out and then place them in the back of the recycling bin where my mom is unlikely to notice them.

I'm not ignoring John's question. I know the answer.

I sit back down and say, "He'd tell me to write her a poem."

John smiles. "A true romantic, huh?"

"Yep."

"Not bad advice, really."

"Maybe not." In my head, I start running through words that might rhyme with Sarah.

"See?" John says, struggling to lift himself from his chair.

I reach over to help him. "What?"

"I told you that love is more interesting than death."

CHAPTER 32

She's (Not) the One

At the coffeehouse the next day, I feel like Madge. I'm writing down words, phrases, sloppy stanzas on the receipts that customers leave behind. Nothing sounds good. I even try my dad's old technique of starting with a line of poetry that I already know and going from there, sort of using it as a creative springboard. Still, nothing.

Frustrated, I tear up the receipts and toss them into the trash can.

"What're you trying to do?" Madge asks me while shaping a tree into the foam of a latte. "Write a poem for Sarah?"

"Jesus Christ," I say, slapping the counter. "Does everybody know?"

"Yes. Well, only the people who matter." She smiles,

pats my cheek.

"Oh, my God." I lean over, bang my head against the counter. Once, twice, three times.

"Relax, Romeo. Murphy told me. And your mom."

"I hate my life."

Madge hands the latte to the woman who's been eavesdropping on our conversation. It's one of the hazards of the job: lack of privacy. Customers loiter at the counter, listening to us talk, as if our lives just might be more interesting than theirs. News flash: They aren't.

When the woman finally wills herself away from the counter and finds a seat well out of earshot, Madge swings around and glares at me. It's a hard, penetrating stare. One full of accusation and, I think, disgust.

"What?" I finally ask, a little petrified.

"Parker," she says, her hands fisted and planted firmly on her hips, "you are a complete idiot."

"What?" I say again, utterly confused.

She rolls her eyes. "Murphy. She likes you. Don't tell me you don't know that."

"I didn't. I don't. Wait...how do you know that? Did she tell you?"

"No," Madge answers, wiping the counter of errant coffee grounds. "I know she likes you the same way she knows you like Sarah. It's called the power of observation. Something that you obviously do not possess."

"Apparently. It must be a superpower that belongs only to women."

"Yep. And don't think we won't use it against you."

I hold up my hands as if I'm about to surrender. "I won't."

The rest of the morning drags. It's busy, but it's the usual crowd. Business owners, bank tellers on breaks, the mayor (without tips), some teachers. (Did you ever run into a teacher over the summer? It's totally weird. It's like seeing an animal out of its natural habitat. Or, is it like seeing them in their element? Either way, it's still strange.) Despite all the busyness, I can't stop thinking about Sarah. And, what's even crazier, I can't stop thinking about what John said, that when it comes to love there's no time like the present.

Look, I tried my dad's advice, or what I assumed would be his advice; but every time I try to write something, the words get all jammed up, like logs in a river. Nothing flows, nothing feels right. "When it comes to wooing women, never underestimate the power of a well-turned phrase," Dad would say. But what if I can't come up with *any* phrase? What then?

After my shift at The Mill is done, I don't walk home. Instead, I head east, toward Sarah's house. She lives in one of the nicest houses in town. It's got a huge front porch that wraps around the side of the house, too. Large, shaggy ferns hang between each column, and bright flowers line the edge of her driveway. Everything at her house is as green and lush as a tropical forest. She even has a swing on the porch that's the size of a twin bed and white, gauzy curtains billowing in the breeze. As I get closer to her street, I can't help but imagine the two of us lounging there. It makes me smile, just thinking about it.

To be honest, I have no idea what I'm going to say, but I

also feel happy, like I'm finally *doing* something, putting my feelings into action. I haven't figured out how this is going to look to Noah and Dante and the others, but I don't care. Not even about Victor right now. It's like I'm being propelled, pushed along by forces greater than myself. I guess that this is maybe what resolve feels like, a hypnotic mix of determination and purpose.

When I step onto Sarah's porch, I'm nervous as hell. The acid in my stomach is roiling, and I feel like I can't catch my breath, not to mention the fact that my palms are sweaty. To put it bluntly: I'm a nervous mess. *There's no time like the present*, I hear John say.

So, I walk toward the door.

But then I spot something through the window. It's Sarah. And Victor.

I lean in a little closer and cup my hand over my eyes. Victor is on the couch, and Sarah is on the coffee table, facing him. She's got her hands on his shoulders. Then she's rubbing his arms. And, worst of all, Victor's crying. I mean, *really* crying. I watch as Sarah reaches for Victor's hands and then leans in to kiss him. It's a tender, lingering kiss. In other words, nothing like the kiss she gave me.

I slink off the porch, guilt and jealousy pushing through my veins.

CHAPTER 33

The Shed...Again

I don't know what I was thinking. I think my talk with John had me stumbling around in a fantasy world, a world in which Sarah would fall into my clumsy arms the minute she saw me. I should have known better. Despite all of Victor's faults, she loves him. And, based on what I saw, he loves her, too, in his own messed up sort of way. I suppose seeing them together, through the fog of her window, saved me from a lot of embarrassment, not to mention all the explaining I'd probably have to do with the guys.

Still, telling myself all of these things doesn't stop me from thinking about her.

The next morning when I tell John about my failed attempt to confess my love to Sarah, he says, "But you didn't actually tell her."

"It would have been pointless," I whine. "Victor was there."

"Well, you're a good friend, anyway." His tone is more conciliatory, as if being a good friend is a distant second to being in love. Based on how I feel right now, he might be right.

It's early in the morning. Very early. I'm up because I have to open The Mill; John's up because he can't sleep. He's taken to falling asleep on the couch at night, kind of propped up a little, because he says this is the only way he feels comfortable enough to fall asleep. My mom used to hate it when my dad fell asleep on the couch, mostly because she hates sleeping alone. It makes me wonder if she's really slept since he died. I doubt it.

"Do you want me to make you anything before I go?" I ask, almost ready to leave. "Bagel? Toast? Anything?"

John rubs at his gut. "No. Thanks." I can't remember when I saw him really eat anything. It seems that food is just poison to him now.

"Well. Bye then," I say as I open the door.

"Bye. Have a good day," he says, trying to hide a groan of pain.

Murphy is already at the coffeehouse when I arrive. My mom's given her a key now, too, like she did with Nils. The key is the ultimate symbol of trust from my mom. You know you're in the inner circle when she hands you a key to her coffeehouse. And Murphy's had hers for a few weeks now. My mom actually asked me if she should give one to Murphy, which really surprised me. It could only mean one of two things: She is beginning to doubt her own sense of judgment, or she is beginning to trust me more. I really hope it's the latter.

When I walk into the coffeehouse, Murphy is struggling with a rather large bag of coffee beans. She's standing on a stepladder so that she is tall enough to actually pour the beans into Bonnie, the grinder. "Hey," I call to her, "you want some help with that?"

"Uh...yeah," she says, putting the bag down on the counter and stepping off the little ladder.

"Why didn't you wait for me?" I ask as I load Bonnie up.

"You know me. I like to be independent. I'm pretty fierce that way, remember?"

I smirk. "Yeah. I remember."

"We haven't worked together in a while. What's up with that?" Murphy wants to know. She's kneeling behind the counter now, turning on the stereo. We don't open for another half hour, so most of the house lights are still off, except for a few pendants near the counter. When Murphy stands up, she's directly under one of the pendant lights. For a moment, it seems like she's the only thing illuminated, like a monument or statue, something important and worth the special lighting.

"What?" she asks, still kind of glowing.

I guess I didn't realize that I was staring at her. "Nothing. Just zoned out for a sec."

"And here I thought you were staring at my boobs. My mistake."

We both laugh. "I think you've been working too much with Charlie," I say. "His sense of humor is rubbing off on you."

"Maybe," she admits, shrugging her shoulders.

And then I turn away and smile to myself because it's so easy with Murphy. Effortless, really. Could that be why Charlie and Madge are on Team Murphy? Maybe. But all I am is confused right now because the easier it is with Murphy, the more I'm reminded about how difficult it is with Sarah.

Then, as if reading my mind, Murphy says, "So...how's Sarah? Have you talked to her yet? Confessed your undying love?"

"No."

"And why not?"

"Because. She's with Victor."

"Uh, yes. Victor the Loser. Such a paradox, he is."

"I think you mean oxymoron."

"Actually, I think I mean asshole."

My mind leaps to the image of Victor helping his dad stumble out of Kelly's. I see him ease his father into the backseat again. I see him on Sarah's couch, a lump of sadness. Not so different from me in some ways. Because, after all, he's kind of fatherless, too. "He's not as bad as you think he is."

"You're defending your rival?"

"He's my friend." My tone is defensive, edged with a little anger, which surprises even me. "And he's had a shitty life," I add.

Murphy looks kind of stricken and holds up her hands, surrendering. "Okay, okay. Sorry." She turns, pretends to straighten up some coffee mugs. "Well, if it's any consolation, I think you're better off. It would've just caused a giant mess for you, anyway."

"I know," I snap. "Can we stop talking about this, please?"

We don't say too much to each other for a while. Thankfully, we are saved by Nils who's come in to drop off his usual breakfast fare: muffins, scones, cinnamon rolls. Today, he's brought a few quiches, too. Already sliced, of course. Before he leaves, he dishes up two slices. "For you," he says with an obnoxious flourish of his arm and a dramatic bow.

"Thanks," we both yell as he walks out through the back. We shove the quiche in our faces, forgoing forks, because it's time to open.

When we open for the day, we are so busy there's no time to talk, except to call out orders to each other. By the way, my mom's developed this new system for calling out orders. Actually, it was a suggestion that my dad had made one night at dinner, and one that my mom was hesitant to use. Until now. Now, I think she's desperate to use any idea he ever had, like it's her way of keeping him alive. Instead of using the customers' actual names, we now have to refer to them as famous characters. When a person places her order, we hand her a card that bears the name of a fictitious character; and when her order's ready, we call out the character's name. My mom let us all choose a handful of names. I chose characters from *Star Wars* and a few from classic literature, like Gatsby. Murphy, of course, chose a bunch from *Harry Potter*. So, nearly every day I find myself yelling, "Severus Snape, your latte is up!"

Today, because Murphy is taking the orders, she gets to decide which characters to assign to our patrons. Needless to say, I've been yelling for Severus Snape, Albus Dumbledore,

Hermione Granger, and, of course, Harry Potter on a fairly steady rotation. And every time I have to yell out one of those names, I notice that Murphy is wearing a big, satisfying grin on her face. I think this is her way of getting back at me for snapping at her earlier.

Finally, when there's a substantial lull, I say, "I'm sorry. I didn't mean to — "

"Be a jerk? I know."

"Any way you might let me call for Luke Skywalker or Han Solo then?"

Murphy taps on her chin with her finger, contemplating my request. Then she says, "I think not."

"How about a character from a different book then?"

"We'll see. Maybe if you're good."

The door opens, and it's Noah and Dante. Their shirts are stained red, so they look as if they've been shot. Multiple times. "I guess it's tough out there in the fields," I say as they approach the counter.

"Yeah," Murphy says, "I feel like we should be thanking you for your service or something."

Dante says, "I know. Every morning, it's an epic battle with the berries."

"And the berries win," Noah adds, holding up his red hands.

Gabe and Tony, who followed the other two in, just give a quick nod hello.

"What do you guys want?" asks Murphy. "You should try the quiche. It's awesome."

"Sure," Noah says.

"Yeah," Dante says, "same."

Gabe and Tony nod again, indicating that they'll have some, too.

After we dish up their food, Noah says, "So, you want to hang out later? We haven't seen you in a while, dude."

"I know. It's just...my mom likes me to be home as much as I can."

"Because of John?" Dante asks.

I nod. This time, it's my turn to be quiet.

"You should hang out with these guys later," a voice behind me says. It's Mom.

"Hey, Mrs. Warren," everybody says in unison.

Mom waves. "Hi, guys. Long time, no see. How are you?"

One by one, they all claim to be good.

"Gabriel and Antonio, how's your mom doing?" My mom always makes it a point to ask about their mom.

"Ella está bien," Gabe answers.

"Yeah, she's good," Tony adds, translating for everyone.

"Glad to hear it," Mom says, gently squeezing Gabe's arm.

"Mom, what about John?" I ask, trying to whisper.

She touches my face and then gives me a peck on the cheek. "You could use some time with your friends, Parker. Really. It's okay. Go hang out in your shack or whatever it is you call it."

"The shed, Mom. The shed."

"Okay, yes. The shed."

It's a cool night, the first truly chilly night of the summer. "Sweatshirt weather" my mom calls it. It's my favorite kind of summer night. One, it gives reason to have a fire; and two, it makes for a good night's sleep. I must admit, I sort of love falling asleep with my hair smelling of burnt pine. My dad used to love a good campfire, too. He'd even get all poetic about it. "Fire is man's greatest paradox," he'd say, taking on a very professorial tone. "It is a symbol of both life and death."

"Couldn't you say the same about water?" I'd pointed out to him one time.

"Yes," he'd said, pleased with my observation. "Yes, you could."

Little did we know that water would be the thing to destroy him.

Tonight, our hopes of having a bonfire have been dashed. Gabe and Tony's mom declined our request to have one in their backyard. It's sort of against the law in town, which she was all too happy to point out to us. I think she must have had visions of her backyard looking something like a forest fire.

"Law, shmaw," Tony had said to his mother.

"Really?" Gabe had asked his brother. "That was your best argument? To *rhyme* at her?"

"I didn't hear *you* coming up with anything better, estúpido."

"¡Cállate la boca!"

To be honest, none of us had a good counter argument. So, we decide to just huddle up in the shed. Yep, all eight of us: me, Dante, Noah, Gabe and Tony, Murphy, Victor, and, of course, Sarah.

Turns out, the shed is a better idea anyway because Dante scored some weed from his brother, who's back in town again. We haven't smoked in a while — well, I haven't at least — so it's nice, passing a joint or two around our circle. It isn't too strong, either. Nice and mellow. I close my eyes and feel like I'm floating, riding a wave to some distant, sandy shore where everything is all palm trees and fruity drinks. Paradise, I guess you could say.

The weed also does a nice job of squelching the urge to stare at Sarah. And her mouth.

We spend most of the evening doing the usual: playing cards, arguing about music, and just talking about whatever, the conversation shifting constantly, like a mouse trying to find its way out of a maze. Noah is the Master of Random Questions. Whenever there's an apparent lull in the conversation, he comes up with another question to keep things moving along. Here's one of them: "What's your guilty pleasure movie?"

Victor jumps in with his answer first. "*Star Wars: Episode 1.*"

"What?!" Dante says, practically choking, little ripples of smoke escaping his lips. "Dude, no."

"I *know*," says Victor, a little mortified at his own admission, a feeling that I'm sure he's unaccustomed to. "But whenever I feel like watching *Star Wars*, for some reason, that's the one I pick."

Tony shakes his head. "You should feel ashamed of yourself."

"Yeah," I add. "You should never admit that to anyone

again."

"C'mon," Victor whines. "It's not *that* bad."

Dante, taking one last drag, says, "It definitely is that bad." When he releases the smoke, it rises above our heads and sits like a fat cumulus cloud before slowly dissipating.

Tony says, "Three words: Jar. Jar. Binks."

Victor leans back, crosses his arms, and says, "Listen, knowing how everything started is important. It *matters*."

"Whoa," I say, "Victor's hitting us with some deep thinking."

Then Murphy chimes in with her usual criticism of all things *Star Wars*. "I don't know why you're all ganging up on Victor. I don't care *what* episode it is."

"Wait a minute," I protest. "You don't even get to have an opinion here, Murph, because you've never watched them."

"Doesn't matter," she says. "I've heard enough about them to form a pretty solid opinion."

"Totally," agrees Sarah. "Anyway, you guys probably just like it because you have weirdo fantasies about Princess Leia in her gold bikini."

"Do you have one?" Noah asks, his tone bordering on creepy.

"Shut up," Sarah says, punching him in the arm.

"Hey, the minute one of you boys starts looking more like Harrison Ford, circa 1980, then we can talk about gold bikinis," Murphy says. Sarah holds up her hand for Murphy to high five, which she does. And just like that, they're allies.

"I knew there was a reason we never used to let girls in here," says Victor, only somewhat kidding.

After a while, my lungs are craving fresh air, so I step out of the shed and lie down in the grass and look up at the stars. A strong wind is moving through the canopy of leaves, and everything feels like it's swirling and twisting and changing direction, like I'm looking through a kaleidoscope.

Then I feel someone beside me. It's Murphy. "What're you doing out here?"

"I just...needed some fresh air."

Murphy moves her arms and legs as if she's trying to make a grass angel or something. "This grass is soft. Like nature's shag carpeting. I could fall asleep here, I think."

"That's just the weed talking."

"Maybe."

"Probably," I whisper, closing my eyes. I move my hand and it brushes against hers, but she doesn't pull it away. In fact, she moves a little closer to me, enough so that our sides are almost touching. I lie still, not sure what to do. I think she wants me to do *something*; at least, that's the message I'm pretty sure she's sending me right now. Otherwise, why would she even be here, lying in the grass next to me?

While I'm still contemplating what to do — kiss her? reach for her hand? get up and leave? — my phone buzzes in my pocket. Murphy sighs a little as I reach for my phone. It's a message from my mom. Taking John to hospital, it says. Meet us there.

CHAPTER 34

I Hate Hospitals

The last time I was at the hospital, it was to identify my dad's body. It was just my mom and me. We spared Hayden the cruelty of having to see Dad just lying there, stiff and waterlogged, his eyes forced shut. I remember my mom clinging to me, like a barnacle to a rock. She just couldn't let go. I think she was afraid that she'd fall.

After she'd told me that he'd died in the lake, we drove to the hospital. Funny, until that moment, I actually never associated hospitals with death. For me, they were always places of hope, places where people went to *get better*, not to die or be dead. Kind of stupid, I know.

My dad was kayaking alone that day. He did that sometimes when he needed to clear his head, but he also just liked Haywood Lake best in the morning, when the water was still cool and motionless. He also liked to kayak away from shore, out past the bay, beyond the steepled shadows of the pines. I know now that he must have been thinking about the letter he'd just slipped into the mail, probably wondering, as he glided over the water, if anything would come of it, if he'd see his father again. I sometimes wonder — okay, I all-the-time wonder — if he was thinking about his father when he felt his heart spasm. And then I wonder how he might have interpreted such a thing, as he tipped over into the water. Would he have thought it ironic? Symbolic? Or would he have just struggled to live? Probably the latter. Still. It was Dad. For him, everything was susceptible to interpretation. Even his own death, if he'd had time enough to think about it.

I think that's what scares me the most sometimes. That he *did* have time to think. That he knew what was happening and could do nothing about it. See, on his death certificate, it doesn't say heart attack as the cause of death. It says drowning. One thing led to the other, of course, but I can't help but wonder what might've happened if he hadn't been on the lake that day. What if he'd just been at home or at the college? What if someone had been there to see him clutch at his chest? Would he be here now? I know I'm not the only one who's been thinking about all these What Ifs. I'm sure they run through my mom's head every day, if not every hour of every day. But it's the What Ifs that cut away at you, like a knife carving out pieces of your soul, shaping you into something different, something unrecognizable.

Or maybe it's the grief that does that. Most likely, it's both. Two blades working at once.

A fisherman found him. He was in a skiff, motoring out to the center of the lake sometime in the early afternoon, when he saw my father's kayak, already capsized. He knew right away that something was wrong, so he jumped in and tried to tip the kayak over. When he finally managed to flip it, he tethered the kayak and my dad to his boat, called 911, and motored in as fast as he could. But it was too late.

"I'm sorry," I remember the fisherman said to us in the hospital. He'd followed the ambulance, hoping that maybe it hadn't been too late. Then, when it very clearly was, he waited, just to see us. I remember that the fisherman was old, mid-seventies maybe, and that he was decked out in all the proper fishing gear: khaki vest with lots of pockets, black hip boots, and a hat that was decorated with hooks and flies that looked more like tiny birds. The hat, though, was in his hands, and I remember that he kept moving it around in a circle. I watched it go round and round, not really hearing what he had to say, except that he was sorry. He said that several times. Not that he had much to be sorry about. After all, he'd tried to save my dad.

So, here I am again. At Haywood Hospital. After reading my mom's text, I ran inside to get Gabe and Tony's mom, who drove me to the hospital. She'd been asleep on the couch, but as soon as she heard me, she leapt up, grabbed her keys, and drove me. No questions asked. (I suspect, however, that there will be plenty of questions for the twins tomorrow, especially about the eau de pot that I'm sure she must have smelled on me.)

When Gabe and Tony's mom dropped me off at the Emergency Room entrance, my mom was waiting in the lobby with Hayden, both of them looking stunned and blurry-eyed. John had already been admitted and was being wheeled up to Radiology for an MRI because Mom had basically ignored John's refusal and demanded that it be done. Hayden told me that John had looked at the doctor and said that it wasn't necessary but that Mom had said, "The hell it isn't," and then got her way.

While John is gone, we sit in the designated waiting room near the lobby. It's a depressing place. The walls are institutional blue and covered with floral prints that might look more appropriate in a nursing home, the kind that smells like mothballs and Lysol. There's a coffee table with a peeling wood veneer and several tattered magazines strewn across its top, ones that should have been thrown out months ago. Someone, in an attempt to make the place look cozy, placed a few fake plants here and there, but even they seem like they'd rather hide in a corner, their tear-shaped, dust-laden leaves drooping with shame.

The wait for John is longer than expected. A couple of hours, at least. Odd since he was supposed to just go up for a scan and then be done. My phone is buzzing constantly. Everyone wants to know if all is okay. Especially Murphy. In more than one of her texts, she offers to come to the hospital, just to sit with me. I tell her no. I do feel bad that I basically bolted on her without saying much of anything.

While I'm sitting here, my mind wanders. It simply refuses to obey me. I keep telling myself to just focus on John, but it won't. Every time I think I have it under control, another thought pops up and I have to try and beat it down, like in one of those stupid arcade games. I want to be *present*, but for some inexplicable reason I find myself imagining the shape of my body pressed into the grass next to Murphy's.

And then I think about Sarah. And Dad. And then Murphy again. It's like my emotions are on some demented playlist with song titles, like "You Can't Always Get What You Want," "Love the One You're With," and "Wish You Were Here."

When John is finally done, they put him in a private room on the second floor. "This can't be good," Hayden whispers as he leans into me.

"Why?"

"Because. Don't you ever watch any hospital shows? A private room means he's gonna be here for a while. It means something *serious*."

"Or it could just mean that he needs some rest."

"No. It's something serious. Trust me." He's still whispering, still leaning against me.

"Well, we already know that he has cancer. How much more serious can it get?"

Hayden stares straight ahead. At what, I don't know. Then he says, "It could mean that...it's getting closer."

John is asleep right now. They're giving him what I can only assume are a bunch of pain meds through an IV. Mom is slumped in a chair near the head of his bed, and Hayden and I are next to each other, on the other side. Mom is reading, or trying to; and Hayden is on his iPad playing some annoying game. I'm just sitting here, quiet, too many thoughts tumbling around in my head.

The nurses try to convince us to go home, but Mom just keeps refusing them, mostly with her steely silence. Finally, she says to one of them, "I'll not have this man wake up alone. When he opens his eyes, he will see us. He has to see us here with him."

By early morning, John finally wakes up. He's groggy but lucid. "Did you all stay through the night?" he says in a hoarse voice.

"Yeah," says Hayden first. "Do you know that you snore?"

John pats Hayden's hand. "So I've been told."

"Have you been told that you sound like a pig jumping out of a plane?"

John laughs, but it's not a funny laugh. It's a sad laugh. It's the kind of laugh that says, *I'm tired and can't think of anything else to say but I know I need to say something so I'll just open my mouth and hope that some sort of noise comes out.*

"That's a very creative description, Hayden," Mom says, retrieving her wallet from her bag. "Here's a few bucks. Why don't you go and get me a cup of coffee from the machine out there in the waiting area."

Hayden takes the money from Mom and says, "You're kidding me."

"I just need caffeine right now. I don't care what it tastes like. And get yourself something, too."

"A candy bar?" he asks, eyebrows lifted.

"Sure," Mom says, lacking the energy to fight with him. "Breakfast of champions."

While Hayden is gone, a doctor steps into the room. She looks very official, wearing a white coat that stops at her knees, a stethoscope flung over her shoulders, and charts tucked under her arm like a permanent accessory. Her hair is kind of messy, though; and her eyes are bloodshot. "Hi," she says, "I'm Dr. Robinson." She shakes everyone's hands and then sits down in the chair where Hayden was sitting.

"I asked the doc here to talk to you two," John says, his eyes glued to the doctor's.

The doctor presses her lips together and then flips open her chart. "So... you are aware that John's cancer has spread. And that it's inoperable." She isn't asking; she's stating.

"Yes," John says, prodding the conversation along.

"Wait. What?" my mom says, suddenly much more alert. "I mean, are you sure?" Her eyes are darting back and forth between John and the doctor. "What about chemotherapy or radiation or both? There's got to be something." She sounds desperate and scared and I'm wishing that I was sitting next to her, just to give her something to hold on to.

But before I can do anything, John reaches for her hand. "Grace, I appreciate what you're trying to do. More than you will ever know. But I've already tried chemotherapy, and it just made me feel sicker."

"But it *worked* before."

"Grace," John interrupts. "Let's hear what the doctor has to say. About what to do now."

Dr. Robinson clears her throat. "Well, for starters, I'd

like to insert a feeding tube. It's a relatively simple procedure."

"Why?" I ask. "I mean, why does he need that?"

"Because," says the doctor, "swallowing and eating food normally isn't really happening anymore, so we need a way to get nutrients to your grandfather."

"But — "

John pats my hand now. "Parker, let her finish," he whispers.

"After that, the most important thing is John's level of comfort. I can help get you set up with hospice so that he can be at home with all of you."

"Wait," Mom says again, shaking her head, trying to take in everything that's being said. "Hospice? Really? My God, he was just outside yesterday gardening." She's out of her chair now, pacing the room, playing with her necklace.

I can guess what my mom is thinking. When you hear the word *hospice*, what you really hear is *the end*.

Dr. Robinson sets her chart down on the bed and rests her hand on John's shin. "I know this isn't easy. For any of you. But things are going to start to *accelerate*, and you'll want to have plans in place for when that starts to happen." The doctor looks directly at my mother and says, "If I really thought there was something else we could do, something else we could try, believe me, I'd be the first to suggest it."

Mom doesn't say anything. She just looks as if she's been punched in the gut.

"I know that you have a lot to talk about, so I'll leave you alone," says Dr. Robinson. "In the meantime, I'm going to get you set up with the OR for the feeding tube." She stands up, gives my shoulder a quick squeeze, and then starts to walk out.

"How long?" my mom asks, staring out the window.

The doctor turns around, slowly. "Maybe a month." She bows her head a little, spins back around on her heels, and then heads out the door, letting the news hang over us.

"Grace," John says, his voice still raspy. "If this is too much, we can figure something else out. We can make other arrangements. I don't have to stay with you." I can tell that this is not an empty offer. He really means it.

Mom says, "Don't be ridiculous. Of course you're staying with us. It's not even a question."

"Besides," I add, "where would you go?"

"Parker, I've spent nearly my entire life figuring out where to go, and I've always landed somewhere."

My mom sits down on the edge of his bed and holds one of his hands in hers. "No more figuring, okay? You've stuck this landing."

Just a few seconds later, Hayden walks in with a coffee and an armful of snacks. Before he can sit down, though, I'm running out of the room, chasing Dr. Robinson down the hall. "Doctor? Dr. Robinson?" I yell. "Wait."

Dr. Robinson turns around, but she doesn't completely stop. She keeps walking, just at a much slower pace. "Parker, right?"

"Yeah," I say, mildly out of breath. "Listen, I'm sorry to bother you. But...doesn't this seem awfully fast? He's been weak, sure. But c'mon. This is his first hospital visit here." The doctor sits down on a bench in the hallway. She waves her arm, inviting me to sit next to her. At first, she's quiet. We are serenaded by the discordant sounds of the hospital: the incessant hum of the fluorescent lights, the intercom barking orders, the determined footfalls of doctors and nurses as they walk in and out of rooms, snapping their charts open and closed. "Parker," she starts, folding her hands on her lap, "your grandfather has been sick for a very long time."

"I know that." Suddenly, I am at the river again, tossing John's rod in the water, clamoring up the hill. I shut my eyes, willing the memory to slink back to where I'd hidden it, somewhere in the deep cranial valleys of my mind.

"He tells me that you all just met recently."

"When did he tell you that?" I ask, seriously trying to figure out when he would have had the time to explain our family's history. Or the lack thereof.

"After his screening. We talked for a bit then."

"Oh," I say, wondering just how much he told her.

"He's been living with this news for a while now, Parker. For you and your mom and your brother, it's still fresh."

"Like you said, we kinda just met, so everything about this is 'still fresh.'"

Dr. Robinson smiles, but it's a doctor's smile, which is to say that it feels rehearsed and somewhat restrained. "You're right. And, considering everything you've been through, I know this can't be easy."

"He told you about my dad?"

Dr. Robinson tilts her head to the side, nods. The universal show of sympathy. "Yes. He told me. And I'm very sorry for you. For all of you."

This time, it's my turn to nod. Then I say, "There's

really nothing else we can do?"

Her shoulders sink a little under the weight of my question. "Let's just say this: He won some battles, but he cannot win this war. I hate that metaphor, but it's the only way I know how to explain it." She stops, folds her hands on her lap again, and turns toward me. "Look, Parker. Cancer is an awful, awful thing, but the one good thing about it — depending on how you look at it, I guess — is that it allows you to say goodbye. It robs you of many things, but it doesn't rob you of that." Then she stands up and says, "I have to go. But remember what I said."

I watch her walk down the hall and through some double doors that swing open for her as if by magic.

There's a part of me, a very large part of me, that knows she's right. Losing my dad so suddenly, it was as if he'd been ripped out of the world. What I wouldn't give to say goodbye to him. To tell him I love him.

Still, there's a small, nagging part of me that doubts the doctor. Yes, I will get to say goodbye to John, the grandfather I've only just met, but all that means is that I will have to watch him die.

CHAPTER 35

A Poetry Reading

Even with the help of a hospice nurse, the task of taking care of John quickly proves to be a full-time job. Dr. Robinson wasn't kidding when she said that things would accelerate. Just a few days after John came home from the hospital, he was bedridden. Kind of. He still gets up to go to the bathroom on his own, but that's about it. The rest of the time, he sleeps or reads Dad's books.

Actually, he devours Dad's books. One after the other. I think it's the only thing that's giving him what little strength he has left.

We decided to set John up in the living room, which is ironic, on many levels. With John's bed smack-dab in the middle of it, and all of the old furniture and books keeping vigil over him, it seems more like a dying room than anything else. Life and death are merging and mixing here, like brackish water.

It's the beginning of August now. I once heard someone describe August as one long Sunday, and I think what he meant was that it's impossible to relax because you keep thinking about how summer's going to end soon and how you haven't done everything you wanted to do before it comes to a halt. Between helping out with John, working at The Mill, and doing some work for all of the AP classes that I stupidly signed up for, August feels more like the crappiest Monday ever.

To be honest, the coffeehouse provides a break. At least there I get to see some of my friends, talk to other people. The house just feels oppressive. With Dad's absence and John's illness, there just isn't air enough to breathe. Death, it seems, has taken over the house. It's everywhere. Crouching in the corners, slinking down the halls, rubbing its back against us like a cat always on the prowl.

Today, Madge, Charlie, Murphy, and I are working the same shift. I think my mom did that on purpose, just to make me happy. I also think that they have made it their mission to make me laugh all day long; and by some miracle, they manage to do it. Charlie, of course, relies on innuendo; Madge, on her gruff, exaggerated disapproval of nearly everything that Charlie says; and Murphy, on her sharp sarcasm. They are seriously on their games today.

And they seriously avoid asking too many questions about John or my dad or my family in general. They are being good friends by trying to let me forget about everything else, even though we all know that it's clinging to me like a bad odor, one that seems impossible to wash away.

With only an hour or so left in our shift, Charlie whispers, "So, when're you going to ask Murphy out?"

"What?"

"C'mon. You should go for it."

"Naw," I say, turning all shades of red.

"And why not?"

"Because...I don't know...it's *Murphy*," I say, as if citing her name were reason enough. For a brief second, I close my eyes and she's lying next to me in the grass again. I can feel her, moving closer, our bodies nearly touching.

Charlie shakes his head in disappointment. "Dude, you need something good in your life. Too much sadness causes shrinkage."

"I thought that was just cold water."

"Nope. I'm telling you, man, depression shrivels the ol' twig and berries."

"Shut up, dude," I laugh, but I also look around, just to make sure that Murphy didn't overhear us. She's at the front of the house near the windows, straightening up some magazines and books. The light is hitting her just right. Her blonde hair is almost shimmering, and her tanned skin is nearly glowing. She really does look beautiful right about now.

She must have felt my staring at her because she turns and looks at me and smiles. And it's not a quick, passing kind of a smile; it's the kind that makes you feel like you're getting someone's full attention, like they're really *seeing* you. And then, just like that, I am sitting in the back of my father's classroom, listening to him read a passage from *The Great*

Gatsby, the one about Gatsby's smile and how it has a "quality of eternal reassurance" and that it possesses "an irresistible prejudice in your favor." He loved that description, and he often quoted it whenever he met someone who possessed a good smile. Dad couldn't help himself that way. His compliments were always given in the context of some literary allusion. "Side effect of the job," he'd say, offering his own genuine smile.

"Are you thinking about taking my advice?" Charlie asks, noticing that I'm staring straight at Murphy who, by the way, is still staring back at me.

I answer honestly. "No. I'm thinking about *The Great Gatsby*."

"God, you're hopeless." But then he adds, "Actually, what you are is your father."

"I'll take that as a compliment," I say, pulling my eyes away from Murphy.

"Good. It was meant to be one."

"What are you two conspiring about over there?" Madge asks while she shapes a flower into the foam of a cappuccino.

And, just to give Charlie a dose of his own medicine, I say, "Oh, we're just trying to figure out the best strategy to use to get you to go out with him."

Charlie just stands there, his mouth agape and his cheeks turning red under his beard. But Madge says, "All he has to do is ask."

"Really?" Charlie says, recovered and hopeful.

"Doesn't mean I'll say yes," smirks Madge.

When our shift is over, Murphy asks if I want to hang

out. I do, but I feel like I should head home. Murphy shrugs and says, "I'll walk with you."

"But what about your car? You'll have to walk all the way back here."

"Nope. My mom dropped me off today. She needed the car to run some errands. I can just have her pick me up at your house."

When she says this, I feel myself get all tense. I haven't had a friend over since my dad died. I'd say it's because they're avoiding my house and all of its sadness, but I'm really the one keeping them away. Not from me. From the house. After all, I hang out with them to *escape* my house. "Sure, yeah," I say, but I'm nervous because I don't know what she expects. Will she want to come in? Will she feel the sadness lurking everywhere and want to run?

I guess there's only one way to find out.

So, we walk to my house. For much of the way, we are quiet. But we don't want to be. I can tell that we are each trying to come up with something clever and playful to say because we keep stealing glances at one another. It's a silence that doesn't just want to be filled with words, though. It wants something more, something better.

When we're almost to my house, Murphy breaks the spell first. "How's it feel?"

"How's what feel?"

"Like, with your dad and now John. How's it feel...you know...trying to handle all of it?"

"It feels...it...I don't know...it sorta feels like I've got a rock in my shoe and I can't get it out."

"Sounds painful. And irritating."

"Yes. It is."

We sit down on the front steps. I notice then that the grass needs mowing, a job we usually reserve for Hayden, except that he's been spending a lot of time with John. There're also about a million weeds growing in the flowerbeds. Some of them have been here for so long, they've already bloomed and shrunk to seed; others, like some creeping vines, have spread more quietly, threading themselves between the rocks that border the landscaping.

Behind us, I hear the door open. It's Mom. "Hey, guys. Murphy, nice to see you. How was the coffeehouse?"

"Busy," I answer.

"Good," Mom says. "You two coming in?"

"Sure," Murphy says, already heading toward the door.

I follow Murphy, anxious about what she might see or hear or feel. "Do you want something to eat?" I ask, trying to push her toward the kitchen and past the living room as quickly as possible.

"No," she says, "I'm good." She stops at the entrance to the living room, points, and asks, "Can I meet him?"

My mom turns around and answers for me. "Of course."

I must be wearing a very terrified look on my face because my mom whispers to me, "Today's a good day, Parker. Don't worry."

John is propped up in his bed. His hair has been brushed, and his face looks ruddy and full. On his lap is a book, which he's taken a break from reading. When he sees us, he says, "Well, Parker, who's your friend?" which fills me with relief. See, he's been confusing some names recently, and I'm afraid that he's going to think that Murphy is someone else. Like Sarah.

"I'm Murphy," she says, holding out her little mitten of a hand.

"Murphy," he repeats, looking a little confused.

"Yes."

"Unusual name."

"Yes. I get that a lot."

"Well," John says, setting his book aside, "better than John. It's much too common."

Murphy smiles. "Common can be good."

"Common is boring." He picks up his book again. "Do you like to read, Murphy?"

"Yes, of course."

"What do you like to read?" John asks, attempting to reach for his glass of water. Murphy lifts it for him, holds the straw to his mouth. "Thank you," he says after he takes a sip.

"I like fantasy stories mostly. I figure I've had too much reality, you know?"

"You can say that again," John says, tugging gently at his IV tubes, which remind me of a den of snakes. But then he picks up the book he'd been reading and hands it to Murphy. "I wonder, Murphy, if you wouldn't mind reading to me for a bit. My eyes are getting a little tired."

Murphy takes the book into her hands, carefully, as if she's accepting a great and rare offering. She turns the book over in her hands and reads the title aloud. "*A Boy's Will* by Robert Frost. Any poem in particular you'd like me to read?"

"Lady's choice," John says, his eyes closed.

I'm afraid that Murphy's going to just get up and leave because this is all too much and too weird. But she doesn't. She opens the book, rolls her thumb along the edges of each page until she finds one that she seems to like. When she starts to read, I recognize the poem. It's "Going for Water," one of Dad's favorites. "A simple, lyrical poem with a little bit of magic," I can hear him say. And the way Murphy's reading it, it does kind of feel like magic.

The well was dry beside the door,
And so we went with pail and can
Across the fields behind the house
To seek the brook if still it ran;

Not loth to have excuse to go,
Because the autumn eve was fair
(Though chill), because the fields were ours,
And by the brook our woods were there.

We ran as if to meet the moon
That slowly dawned behind the trees,
The barren boughs without the leaves,
Without the birds, without the breeze.

But once within the wood, we paused
Like gnomes that hid us from the moon,
Ready to run to hiding new
With laughter when she found us soon.

Each laid on other a staying hand
To listen ere we dared to look,
And in the hush we joined to make
We heard, we knew we heard the brook.

A note as from a single place,
A slender tinkling fall that made
Now drops that floated on the pool
Like pearls, and now a silver blade.

By the third stanza, I feel hypnotized. There's an unexpected softness to Murphy's voice as it glides over the words, and they feel like silk, sort of caressing my ear. And as she finishes the last stanza, I notice that John has fallen fast asleep.

Murphy closes the book and sets it on the table next to John's bed. Then, as if she's known him forever, she reaches over and touches his hand, even gives it a little squeeze.

"Thank you," I whisper, "that was really...beautiful."

"You're welcome." She's standing in front of me, waiting for what I'm not sure I have the courage to do.

Luckily (or not), there's a knock at the door. It's Murphy's mom.

"I have to go," she says, still looking up at me.

"I know." We can hear our moms talking on the porch, but we can't unlock our eyes.

"Murphy," my mom calls, "your mom is here."

And just like that, the trance is broken. I walk Murphy

to the door and we wave an awkward goodbye.

When they drive away, I go back into the living room and sit next to John. "Well," he says, his eyes still closed, "you blew that chance, didn't you?"

"I thought you were asleep!"

"I faked it."

"What?"

"I faked it. I wanted to see if your dad's theory about wooing women with poetry really worked."

"But she read to *you*! I didn't read to her."

"So you *do* like her."

"Oh, my God," I mutter, slapping myself in the forehead.

"Hey," John coughs, trying to prop himself up a little, "I was just trying to help you out. I was trying to be your wingman."

All this meddling into my lackluster love life is beginning to take its toll. I'm starting to think I need a girlfriend just so people will stop harassing me, or so I won't seem so pathetic to myself (and to everyone else). "I don't need any help," I say, adjusting a pillow for him.

"You're probably right about that. I think Murphy likes you back. Just one move from you and she'll fall right into your arms."

"How can you tell?"

"Parker, she read a poem to a dying man she just met. She didn't do that for me. She did it for you."

We spend the rest of the evening talking and reading. Mom and Hayden join us, too, for dinner. It seems cruel to eat in front of him, but he insists that we not feel guilty. In fact, he says that even though he can't eat the food, he can still enjoy the sight and smell of it, anyway.

    I'll admit, though, my mind is distracted as usual. I keep thinking about the moon dawning behind the trees and the drops of water becoming the silver blade of a river.

CHAPTER 36

Running Out of Time

The hospice nurse, Renee, reminds me of a female Ronald McDonald. She has a head of red, puffy hair, and she tends to wear a lot of yellow or red scrubs. She also wears glasses that take up about half of her face. She may also be the nicest, most patient person I've ever met. She seasons her sentences with too many terms of endearment, something that would have driven my dad crazy, but I don't really mind it. She's a caretaker. Her default is kindness.

Anyway, Renee is here to feed John through his tube. She's here every day in the morning — feeding him, changing his IV, checking his pain levels — then she gives updates to Dr. Robinson, who's also stopped by a couple of times herself. That's the perk of a small-town hospital, I guess. The doctor will still sometimes come to you. Medical bag and all.

"Honey," Renee says to me. "I'm having a little trouble today with the feeding tube. I think there might be an infection around where it's inserted. And your grandpa seems a little more uncomfortable than usual, so I'm gonna give the doctor a call and have her stop by later. Okay, sweetheart?"

"Okay." What else do I say?

When Dr. Robinson arrives later in the afternoon, she talks to John first, just the two of them, then she comes into the kitchen and sits at the table where we've been waiting. "Are you off the clock yet?" my mom asks.

The doctor takes a peek at her watch. "Yes, I believe I am."

"Wine?" Mom asks, holding up a bottle.

"Um...I probably shouldn't — "

"Do I need to remind you that my husband just died and now I have his father — you know, the man he didn't see for almost thirty years — in my living room, *dying*?" My mom is angry, not at the doctor, just at everything. Right now, she's practically daring the doctor to say no to her.

"Okay," Dr. Robinson relents. "But just half a glass."

After my mom pours the wine, the doctor says, "John's body is starting to reject the feedings. It won't be long before things start shutting down."

"How long?" Hayden asks. He's scared of losing John, but he's also scared of losing Dad all over again. See, John has been telling Hayden story after story after story about Dad, giving him anything and everything he can remember. And Hayden is writing all of it down in black Moleskine notebooks. Truth is, there is a constant back and forth between John and all of us. We are giving him his son, but he is giving us our dad. Losing him means that all of this sharing will stop and that we'll all have to go back to just thinking about what we used to have.

"A few days. A week, if we're lucky." The doctor takes a sip of her wine, waits for our reaction.

"What do we do now?" Mom asks, trying desperately to hold back the tears that are threatening to slip down her cheek.

"Manage his pain. Make him as comfortable as possible. I have to warn you, though, keeping him lucid will be difficult. He may get confused at times. The most important thing is to say what you need to say. Say your goodbyes, and say them when you know he can hear them."

The doctor leaves before finishing her glass of wine. Mom picks it up and pours the rest of it into her own glass. The three of us sit at the table, quiet and still, Dad's empty chair staring at us.

And John in the other room, dying.

CHAPTER 37

Everything Merges into One

So, John has asked me to read *A River Runs through It* to him. Like I said before, I never cared much for the book, but several pages into it, I can see why John likes it so much. It's about a family that loves each other, but it's got its troubles. A son whose risky behavior ends up getting him killed, and a father and older brother who can't understand him but love him despite all of his mistakes. In John's case, the roles are reversed, but does it really matter? The point is the same: unconditional love.

If you've never read it, though, the long-winded descriptions of fly fishing can be really boring. Somehow, though, I think these might be John's favorite parts. He loves the descriptions of the flies and the casting techniques and the imagery of the river. I suspect that he's being transported in his own mind to some river — maybe even the Glendale River — imagining that he's knee-deep in fast currents and hoping that he doesn't catch his line in the leafy bough of a tree that's hanging a bit too low for a fisherman's liking.

I read off and on throughout the afternoon in between his naps. Sometimes he falls asleep while I'm reading. A few times, he mutters, "Jack, Jackie," and I think that maybe he still wants to talk to Hayden, to finish telling him some stories. But Hayden is done asking him questions. He's just been lying alongside him on his bed, sort of whispering in his ear. Saying his goodbyes.

At some point, maybe around midnight, I fall asleep reading the book.

I wake up in the morning with the book resting on my chest, its edges curled up so that it looks like a soaring bird. Hayden is next to me, sleeping on the floor.

"Jack?" I hear John whisper. "The river."

I think that maybe he wants to hear the end of the book, so I open it and read. When I get to the last couple of paragraphs, I see my mom. She's standing in the foyer, just outside of the living room, where I was standing when John first arrived here. And, like me, she looks like maybe she doesn't want to come in. I pause for just a moment and then read: "Eventually, all things merge into one, and a river runs through it. The river was cut by the world's great flood and runs over rocks from the basement of time. On some of the rocks are timeless raindrops. Under the rocks are the words, and some of the words are theirs." Before I read the very last line, I look over at my mom, who is silently crying. Then I whisper, "I am haunted by waters."

I close the book and set it down on the bed. "Jack," John says, opening his eyes, looking at me. "Jackie, let's go fishing. Let's go down to the river."

By now, Hayden has woken up and is sitting next to me, leaning his head against my shoulder, watching John breathe.

"Jack?" John says again, his voice scratchy and distant.

I start to shake my head like I'm about to correct him when my mom finally steps into the room. She sits down next to Hayden and gives me a prodding nod. I know what she wants me to do.

"Dad," I whisper, "I'm here. I'm right here."

John grabs my hand and holds it, squeezing it with whatever residual strength he's got left. "Jackie, I'm sorry. I'm sorry I left you."

"I know, Dad," I say. "I know."

He's looking at me and Hayden and Mom. He's reaching for all of us. "I love you, Jack," he says. He's struggling now, fighting for air.

"I love you, too, Dad," I whisper. "I love you, too."

He swallows one last, labored breath, and then he's gone.

And then, with what's left of my family sitting beside me, I do what I should have done a long time ago, what I should have done when my dad died.

I cry.

CHAPTER 38

John's Funeral

The day after John died, hospice cleared everything out. The bed, the IVs, the meds. All of it, just gone. The dying room is now a living room again. Sort of. It's still filled with all of Dad's books that Hayden and I brought down for John to read. Even Dad's journals, which Hayden shared with John, are still here. The old man read every single one of them. In the end, I think he knew his son pretty well.

Over the next couple of days, we begin the slow, sad process of carrying everything back up to the attic. I tell Mom that she doesn't have to help, but she insists, even though I know the thought of going up there still scares her. When she first steps into Dad's office, she just stands there, kind of like John did when he first saw it. She looks around, a stack of books cradled in her arms, and takes a few deep, long breaths, as if she's just broken the surface of the water.

"Dusty almonds," she whispers, smiling at me. And I smile back.

When she and Hayden head downstairs after carrying up the last of Dad's books, I decide to hang back and organize his journals, placing them once again in his old toolbox. It's impossible not to read some of them, so I pick a random one from the pile. It's from 1987. I do some quick math in my head, figuring that Dad would've been about sixteen then. I flip to a couple different pages. As usual, there're doodles and quotes and failed attempts at poems with entire stanzas that have been scratched out, but there is one entry that catches my eye, and so I read it.

July 15, 1987

Today was a good day. Dad came home and we went fishing. We didn't say much, but I liked just sitting with him, listening to the birds and the waves and the sound of the reel. It was so peaceful. There was no one else on the river. Just us.

It felt like everything was ours: the sky, the water, the whole day. I wanted to tell him that I wish we had more days like this, but I didn't. I was afraid he might take it the wrong way and think I was criticizing him for not being around when all I really wanted him to know is that I just miss him.

I close the journal, my thumb still marking the page, and

lean back against the shelf. I look around my dad's office: at his sad, slouching couch, at his desk that's now covered in a thick layer of dust, at his crooked columns of books. I read the entry one more time before I place the journal in the toolbox, thinking that my dad was always best at finding the right words.

Because, yeah, I just miss him.

On the day of John's funeral, it is warm and sunny, unlike Dad's when everything was cold and gray and covered in frost. Also, unlike Dad's funeral, everything has already been planned. I suppose one advantage to knowing that you are going to die in the very near future is that you have a say over what's going to happen at your own funeral. Basically, you compose the music; everyone else just conducts it.

John had made it very clear to my mom that he didn't want a long service. "Short and sweet, like my stay with you," he'd said, patting her on the hand. He also told us that he wished to be cremated. When Mom asked him why, he said, "I've never liked the idea of taking up too much space. Why start after I'm gone?" His only other request was that some of his ashes be buried near his son. "I know it's...a lot to ask, but if you aren't opposed...." There was no opposing. Mom said that she was sure that's what Dad would have wanted.

When we arrive at Haywood Cemetery, we park our car at the bottom of the hill and walk up, taking our time. Mom is in the middle of Hayden and me, holding our hands, pulling us along as if we were still little and crossing a busy street. Behind us trail of some of our friends: Leo and Charlie, Murphy and

Noah and Dante, Gabe and Tony and their mom, and a few of my dad's colleagues. We told them that they didn't have to come, but they'd insisted. Not so much for John, but for us.

At the top of the hill, we form a quiet half-circle around my father's grave and the small hole that's already been dug and then covered by a conspicuous green tarp. Most of John's ashes, which we chose to put in the wooden toolbox that held Dad's journals, are resting atop a small table that's also been draped in some sort of green material. John had told us that he didn't want one of those fancy, shellacked boxes. "I really don't mind if it's nothing more than a shoebox," he'd said. I think he'd be happy to know that we chose *this* box.

Hayden and I each take our turn reading something. Actually, Hayden doesn't read. He just talks for a few minutes, recounting some of the stories that John had told him, even ones about our dad. In some ways, it sort of feels like Dad's funeral all over again, despite the warm weather. The grass on my father's grave is still new and soft and a lighter shade of green than the older grass surrounding it, but it's beginning to turn darker and thicker in some spots. The copper plaque on his headstone has begun to turn a little green, too. It's another cruel reminder that life changes, even for the dead.

When it's my turn, I don't just talk. I read. I read the last passage from *A River Runs through It*. I don't look up — I can't — but I hear a dirge of sniffles and stifled sobs. The last line is nearly impossible to say. It catches in my throat, kind of like a fly hook in an overhanging limb, and I can't seem to tug it free. Finally, I close the book and whisper the last line, just as I did before John died. "I am haunted by waters."

I feel someone grab my hand and I think that it must be my mother again, except that it's much smaller, kind of like a little pebble pushing against my palm. When I open my eyes, I see Murphy beside me. "That was beautiful," she says, squeezing my hand.

"Thank you," I say, squeezing back.

Mom, Hayden, and I each put a hand on the toolbox that once held Dad's words and now holds my grandfather's ashes. Then Mom kneels near Dad's headstone and caresses it, just for a moment. "I miss you," she whispers before pulling us toward her. A family hug, minus two.

CHAPTER 39

John's Truck

Mom, in a fit of generosity, lets me keep John's truck. I've never thought of myself as much of a truck-driving kind of guy, but it feels right, driving his truck around. It feels like there's still a part of him here, you know?

This afternoon I decide to clean out the truck, not that it's much of a mess. In the bed of the truck, there are a couple of metal toolboxes, which I just take out and place in the garage for now. "Can I have these?" Hayden asks, pointing at the toolboxes, already kneeling down to check them out.

"Sure," I answer. "What're you going to do with all the tools?"

"I don't know. Build something, I guess. What else do you do with tools?"

"What do you want to build?"

"I don't know." He's already rifling through one box, pulling out screwdrivers and hammers and a bunch of different chisels.

"Well," I say, "when you figure out what you want to build, we can do it together."

"Really?" He's smiling.

"Sure," I answer, feeling all big-brotherly.

While Hayden continues organizing John's old tools, I turn my attention to the cab of the truck. There are a few old receipts stuffed into the cup holders along with some loose change and a handful of Tums, and there's a collection of roadmaps behind the seat, probably left over from his days of moving around all of the time. *Gypsy carpenter,* I think to myself, smiling. I open the glove compartment and find the usual stuff in there: insurance information, registration, manual to the truck, even the title. Then, underneath everything, I find a large envelope, and it's got our names on it.

I open it and pull out a stack of papers. It's John's will.

I jump out the truck and run into the house to show my mom. We sit at the kitchen table. Well, she sits and I hover over her shoulder. "Holy shit," she says, leaning back in her chair.

"What?"

"It looks like he's left us everything."

"What do you mean 'everything'?"

"He sold his house and his land in Pennsylvania and left us the money." She's covering her mouth. I think she's trying to hide the fact that she's smiling.

"How much?"

She looks at it again. "Three hundred thousand."

"Really?"

"Yes."

"Whoa."

"I know," she says, laughing in disbelief.

"But...when did he...?"

"Sell his house? I don't know. He must've done it while he was here, I guess." Mom stands up and stuffs the papers back into their envelope. "I'll make an appointment with the lawyer to go over all of this." She heads down the hall toward her office, presumably to call the lawyer, but then she comes back and hugs me. "We're going to be all right, Parker."

"Yeah," I whisper.

"You didn't find any other surprises, did you?"

"Nope. Just that."

She smiles, but just with her eyes. "Okay then."

But I did find something else. I found the copy of the Wendell Berry book, *Openings*, that my dad had given John so many years ago. It was in the glove compartment, too. But the book I want to keep for myself.

CHAPTER 40

Still Water

It's the last week of August, and another school year is looming like a storm cloud. You'd think I might be a little more excited, considering that it's going to be my senior year and all. But I'm not. Senior year just means it's the beginning of another ending. It's a long, drawn-out goodbye. And, quite frankly, I'm getting pretty tired of goodbyes. Even the harmless ones, the ones that really just mean *See you later*.

Charlie had to head back to college the other day. I always hate to see him leave, but this time it was especially hard because it's his senior year, too, which means he'll be looking for a real job next spring and no longer harassing me at The Mill. "C'mon," he said, "I'll be around. And you know you can call me whenever you need any dating advice."

I said, "Think I'll pass on that one."

"It's good to see you smiling again, bro. Really."

"Thanks," I said.

Just before he walked out the door, he turned around and said, "Keep an eye on Madge for me, okay?"

"I always do."

The truth is, though, that it will be rather difficult to keep a watchful eye on Madge because she's leaving us, too. Remember the day when I saw her leave The Mill in a suit, or what I thought was a suit? Turns out she had an interview in the city. "It's an internship at *Lark Magazine*. Professor Warren was the one who actually set it up for me, but I put it off when he died because I didn't want to leave then," she'd told my mom. "I'll be editing their fiction and poetry. Well, working with the editors, anyway."

"That's wonderful, Madge. Really," Mom said, hugging her.

So, yeah. I am tired of goodbyes.

I've been spending a lot of my free time just driving around in John's truck. It's best in the evening when the air has begun to cool and I can just put the windows down and feel the wind whipping past me. Sometimes, on the roads that stretch for miles, flat and flanked by fields, I go as fast as I can. I feel like I'm flying.

This afternoon I drove out to Glendale to pick up Murphy. I told her that I wanted to go to Haywood Lake. "Are you sure?" she asked earlier while trying her hand at foam art. "You don't think you'll be too upset being there?"

"I need to go," I told her. And I do. It's time. I just

know I can't go there *by myself*.

On our way to the lake, we are mostly quiet. We don't even turn on the radio. It's enough to feel the wind and hear the gravel grind under the tires. Occasionally, Murphy looks at me and offers a reassuring smile.

When we reach the lake, I drive down a narrow road toward the water, the same road my dad would have driven down that morning. The road is cracked and crumbling along its edges, and it's riddled with so many potholes that you have to weave your way down it. It's also very dark and shaded by trees whose limbs reach over it and nearly touch each other, forming a natural arbor. There's a small parking lot, one that kayakers and fishermen mostly use, at the end of the road. Thankfully, no one else is here. Just us.

A small hill separates the parking lot from the water, but there are steps that someone at some time made from giant slabs of shale and leftover railroad ties. We walk down them, trying to avoid the ties that are noticeably soft with rot and the shale that's flaking a little too much. There's a small dock and a little beach area, if you can call it that. Duckweed rims the edge of the lake here, like someone's thrown buckets of lime-green confetti into the water. There are also long scarves of algae looped around the dock's posts, and patches of moss where the light probably never reaches. On the beach there are the remnants of a campfire enclosed by a crooked ring of stones.

"I like it here. It's peaceful," Murphy says as we sit down on the dock.

"Yeah. That's what my dad thought."

There's really no wind, so the water is very still, the only ripples coming from a few fish that risk swimming near the surface of the water.

"I'll be right back," I say.

"Okay."

I head back up the stairs and grab my backpack. When I make my way back to the dock, Murphy asks, "What's in the bag?"

"You'll see."

I open my backpack and pull out a small blanket. Murphy gives me a quick smirk. "A blanket? Did you have some sort of ulterior motive bringing me all the way out here?"

"No," I say, fighting a smile.

"Hm. Too bad."

"Okay. Now you're just messing with me."

She throws a shoulder into me, gently. "Maybe." She unfolds the blanket and sits back down. I sit next to her. "Anything else in there?" she asks.

I pull out a small glass jar and my copy of *Openings,* and then I set them down between us.

"What's in the jar?" Murphy asks, but I think she already knows.

"Some of my grandfather's ashes."

"Oh," she nods.

"This was one of my dad's favorite places, so I thought it might be good to spread some of his ashes here, too." As I'm talking, I'm starting to doubt myself, like hearing the idea out loud for the first time makes it sound kind of dumb and pathetic. "Is that weird?" I want to know, desperate for

Murphy to tell me it isn't.

"Not at all. I think it's perfect."

I twist the top from the jar, but it's difficult because my hands are shaking. I step to the edge of the dock, ready to spill what's left of my grandfather into the lake, ready to let it swallow a part of him, too.

Murphy is next to me. I can feel her warm breath against my shoulder. She's reading. At first, I just hear sounds, not words. My brain can't — or won't — figure them out. Then, finally, like a switch that's been flipped, I realize that she's reading "The Peace of Wild Things." And just like that day when she read to John, I am entranced. It's almost too much, like euphoria and despair are fighting one another, duking it out over possession of my heart. If I didn't have Murphy to lean against, I might fall right into the lake.

"Wait," I hear myself suddenly whisper, still clutching John's ashes to my chest. "Can you start over?"

Murphy holds the book a little closer to me, and we read the poem together.

> *When despair for the world grows in me*
> *and I wake in the night at the least sound*
> *in fear of what my life and my children's lives may be,*
> *I go and lie down where the wood drake*
> *rests in his beauty on the water, and the great heron feeds.*
> *I come into the peace of wild things*
> *who do not tax their lives with forethought*
> *of grief. I come into the presence of still water.*
> *And I feel above me the day-blind stars*

waiting with their light. For a time
I rest in the grace of the world, and am free.

I like the way Murphy's voice merges with mine, rising and falling to the lilting rhythm of the words. When we're done, Murphy closes the book and touches my arm, nudging me a little.

I tip the jar upside down, and we both watch, expecting John's ashes to find their way to the lake. But they don't. Not at first. They are so fine that they catch on a nearly imperceptible current of wind and float through the air, moving in a little rippling cloud before settling on the surface of the still water.

THE END

ACKNOWLEDGMENTS

A big shoutout goes to my friends and colleagues Jan Freeman, Tricia Janes, Shawna Benzan, Karen Jones, Kayla Rosenbeck, Evan Giacomini, and Sara Cinquino for their time, feedback, and encouragement. Their suggestions and kind words were enough to keep me afloat.

Thank you to my son, Evan, who read the very first draft of the novel and said (and I'm quoting him here), "This sounds like John Green." I definitely did *not* deserve such high praise, but it gave me what I needed to keep going.

Lots of gratitude goes to my husband, John, for giving me the time and space to dream big.

And, finally, to my students, I just want to say this: I see you. I hear you. I love you.

ABOUT THE AUTHOR

Elizabeth Dickhut is a high school English teacher in Western New York. Some of her poetry has appeared in *Boston Literary Magazine*, *Journal of Medical Humanities*, *The Oak Orchard Review*, *The Buffalo News*, and *Artvoice*. She lives with her husband, John, and son, Evan.

Made in United States
North Haven, CT
23 October 2024